WHAT'S WISHED

(A Peyton Risk Suspense Thriller —Book 3)

Ella Swift

Ella Swift

Ella Swift is author of the PEYTON RISK mystery series, comprising five books (and counting).

An avid reader and lifelong fan of the mystery and thriller genres, Ella loves to hear from you, so please feel free to visit ellaswiftauthor.com to learn more and stay in touch.

ISBN: 978-1-0943-8387-3

BOOKS BY ELLA SWIFT

PEYTON RISK MYSTERY SERIES

WHAT'S HIS (Book #1)

WHAT'S LEFT (Book #2)

WHAT'S WISHED (Book #3)

WHAT'S GONE (Book #4)

WHAT'S MINE (Book #5)

PROLOGUE

Amanda stood precariously on the edge of the rugged cliff, her disheveled hair blowing in the wind like tendrils of fear wrapping around her face. The river far below roared and churned, but she was too scared to look down. Her body trembled as she shivered against the cold, early morning air.

How in the world did I get here? she wondered.

Amanda's journey from her humble beginnings had been marked by her passion for the wilderness. At thirty-four years old, she was a park ranger and an unabashed ambassador for the department. Her dedication to her career was unwavering, fueled by an adventurous spirit and an aspiration to help preserve what remained of the world's wildernesses.

Right now, however, the only kind of preservation she was thinking about was self-preservation.

"Please," she whispered, her breath creating a faint mist in the chilly air. "I don't want to die."

Her heart raced as she felt a cold, firm hand nudging her back. She tried to turn around, but the man's voice cut through the air like a razor-edged knife. "Keep your eyes forward."

"Please," she begged, her voice cracking. "Why are you doing this?"

"Everything will make sense later." His words were hollow, void of any empathy.

Desperation clawed at her throat as Amanda attempted to appeal to his humanity. "Think about my family. I've already lost a brother, and my death on top of his would drown them in grief. Please, don't do this."

The man remained silent, his presence looming behind her like an ominous shadow. Amanda's body trembled from both fear and the biting cold that enveloped her. Instinctively, her arms wrapped around herself, providing little comfort against the frigid air.

This can't be real, she thought. She wanted to just close her eyes and wish it all away, like she had as a child when her nightmares became too much to bear. But she knew this was no dream. It was a nightmare come to life.

Mustering every ounce of courage left within her, she forced herself to look down at the river below.

Raging waters churned beneath her, the torrential current carving its way through the rocky landscape. Whitecaps frothed and crashed against boulders, only to be swallowed by the relentless force of the river. The sight intensified her fear, making her stomach churn with dread.

Could she possibly survive such a fall?

As the icy wind stung her cheeks, Amanda closed her eyes for a brief moment, trying to calm her racing thoughts. Survival seemed impossible, but if she could somehow find a way, maybe she could escape this nightmare. It was a slim chance, but it was all she had left to cling to.

"Time's up," the man growled, impatience lacing his voice. "Jump."

Amanda's breath hitched in her throat. "I can't," she whispered, her voice barely audible over the roaring river below.

The man's frustration boiled over. "You have no choice! I'll kill you if you don't jump!"

"Please," she begged, tears streaming down her face. "I'll probably die from the fall anyway. Just let me go."

In a daring move, she began to turn around, hoping that if she could look into his eyes, she might find some shred of mercy. But before she could catch a glimpse of his face, a forceful shove sent her careening off the edge of the cliff.

As Amanda plummeted through the air, her limbs flailed wildly, her stomach lurching with each terrifying second of descent. The wind howled around her like a vengeful spirit, tearing at her clothes and hair as if to hasten her demise. Her heart pounded against her chest, threatening to burst from the sheer terror coursing through her veins.

Her body collided with the icy river below, shattering the water's surface with an explosive splash. The shock of the frigid water engulfed her, searing every nerve ending and leaving her disoriented and gasping for air. Panic clawed at her mind, but she knew she had to focus if she wanted any chance of surviving this nightmare.

Amanda's lungs burned as she fought to keep her head above the water, its icy grip threatening to swallow her whole. The relentless current churned around her like a ravenous beast, clawing at her limbs and dragging her deeper into its watery domain.

"Help!" she screamed, her voice barely rising above the roar of the river. But there was no one nearby to hear her desperate plea, only the mocking silence of the wilderness.

Her arms flailed in the water, a futile attempt to gain some semblance of control over her situation. Panic bubbled up inside her, threatening to consume her entirely. All she could think about was drowning, the cold darkness of the depths calling her name.

It can't end like this. Not like this. Whatever happens, I'm not giving up.

As if in response to her determination, the sound of crashing water reached her ears. She turned her head downstream, and her heart dropped. A waterfall loomed before her, frothy, foaming waves that disappeared over an edge she couldn't see but could hear all too well.

No, no, no! she thought, her eyes wide with terror. Desperate, she kicked and thrashed against the current, her muscles screaming in protest as she tried to swim upstream. But it was no use—the river's grip was too strong, its pull too powerful for her weakening body to overcome.

Come on, fight it! she urged herself, pushing past the exhaustion that threatened to claim her consciousness. But despite her best efforts, she couldn't deny the truth: She was growing weaker by the second, and the waterfall drew ever closer.

A sudden memory of her mother's soothing voice pierced through Amanda's panic. *Breathe, sweetheart. Slow and steady. You can handle anything life throws at you.* The memory brought with it a fleeting moment of calm, allowing Amanda to gather her thoughts.

"Mom..." she whispered, trying to find her center. Her heart rate steadied as she realized that fighting against the river current was futile. Instead, she needed to use it to her advantage. She glanced over at the bank, where a gnarled old tree stood defiantly against the water's assault. Its twisted branches stretched out over the river like the arms of a protective guardian.

Maybe... maybe I can reach it, she thought, hope bubbling up within her. With newfound determination, she angled herself toward the tree and began swimming with the current, aiming for one of the lower branches.

There was a loud splash behind her, but she dared not look back. She told herself the man was just throwing rocks at her—he had probably assumed she would drown, and now he was desperate to end her life before she escaped. All she had to do was get beneath the cover of the trees, and all would be well.

The icy water clawed at her skin like a thousand frozen daggers, but she forced herself to swim faster, harder. Her breaths came in short, panicked gasps as the gnarled tree drew closer and closer. She could almost reach the outstretched branches that seemed to beckon her to safety.

"Come on, come on," she whispered to herself, desperation fueling her every stroke. "Just a little farther."

Her fingertips grazed one of the branches, but it slipped away from her grasp. A strangled cry escaped her lips as she lunged for it again, her heart pounding in her ears. This time, she managed to wrap her trembling fingers around the rough bark and clung to it as if her life depended on it—which, of course, it did.

With agonizing slowness, she began to pull herself toward shore, the relentless current fighting her every step of the way. When her feet finally touched the sandy bottom, she nearly sobbed with relief. *Just a few more steps,* she thought, *and I'll be free.*

But just as she started to believe she might actually escape, a powerful hand closed around her wrist from behind, wrenching her back into the freezing embrace of the river. She screamed, her terror raw and primal, and tried to fight the man off, her other hand flailing wildly against his iron grip.

"Let me go!" she cried as the man pulled her under the surface once more. The world went dark and silent as the water enveloped her, and she heard nothing but the roar of the river and the frantic pounding of her own heart.

CHAPTER ONE

Ranger Peyton Risk sat stiffly at her computer, her knuckles white as they gripped the edge of the desk. The audio recording crackled to life through the speakers, her late father's voice piercing the silence of her small cabin home.

"Rex," he said urgently, using the name of the ranger to whom he'd sent the recording, "I don't have much time. Someone's coming after me. I can feel it in my bones. I just wanted you to know in case something happens to me."

Peyton's heart clenched as she listened, feeling the weight of her father's words deep within her chest. Her dark eyes were wide with concern, and her brow furrowed as she tried to decipher the cryptic message. She had listened to this recording countless times, hoping to find a clue or some new insight into her father's – and her mother's – untimely deaths.

The early morning light filtered through the curtains, casting a warm glow on the wooden walls of the cabin. Peyton was still dressed in her pajamas, a testament to how little sleep she had gotten since discovering the recording. A mug of now-cold coffee sat beside her computer, forgotten in her pursuit for answers.

Her surroundings were simple but comforting. The cabin was filled with mementos of her childhood with her parents, Galen and Marie Risk. An intricately carved wooden shelf held a collection of dusty books, their spines worn from years of use. Paintings created by her talented mother adorned the walls, capturing the vibrant beauty of Eden's Gate National Park, where her family had often spent their weekends camping together. It was bittersweet; every corner of the cabin held memories of the loving, adventurous parents who had been taken from her sixteen years ago in that very park. The crime remained unsolved, haunting her to this day.

Peyton forced herself to focus on the recording, blocking out the painful memories that threatened to consume her. She strained to hear any background noise or a clue that she might have missed in her previous listens. Her father's voice continued, his tone increasingly desperate.

As the recording played on, her father's voice grew increasingly more somber. "I'm in danger, Rex," he said. "It's my work, I know it. I never wanted to involve Peyton or Marie in this mess, but now I don't have a choice."

Peyton's brow furrowed as she took in this new information. She had always known her father as a skilled carpenter, the very one who built the cabin she now called home. But what other work could he have been involved in that would put his life at risk? The realization dawned upon her that there was so much about her father that she didn't know.

"I may have to head to the Red Pine Cabin," her father continued. "It's tucked away in the heart of Sprucewood Park, among the oldest red pines in the area. The cabin is camouflaged by the surrounding trees, making it near impossible to find unless you know where to look."

Peyton's heart raced as she listened to her father's description of the mysterious Red Pine Cabin. She couldn't recall ever hearing about such a place during their numerous camping trips to Sprucewood Park. Desperate to locate the cabin and uncover her father's secrets, she felt an overwhelming sense of frustration at not knowing where to start.

Sprucewood Park is vast, she thought to herself. *How can I possibly find this cabin without any clear directions?*

She opened her browser and began typing with determined keystrokes: "Red Pine Cabin, Sprucewood Park." Her heart raced with anticipation, hoping for a clue to lead her to the mysterious place her father had mentioned.

Search result after search result popped up on the screen—pictures of cozy Airbnbs adorned with twinkling fairy lights and luxurious amenities. One boasted a private hot tub with views of the surrounding forest, while another flaunted a modern interior with floor-to-ceiling windows. None of these seemed relevant to the cryptic message in her father's recording.

"Think, Peyton," she muttered to herself, racking her brain for any other possible way to find the Red Pine Cabin. She knew it wouldn't be as simple as finding a cabin listed on Airbnb, but it was the only starting point she had.

As she scrolled aimlessly through the search results, her thoughts drifted to the storage unit where she had placed her parents' belongings while she remodeled their cabin, which had fallen into disrepair in the years since their deaths. The items were mainly a hodgepodge of sentimental trinkets and memorabilia, but there were also photo albums filled with happy memories of family vacations and Christmases, a wooden jewelry box that had once belonged to her mother, and a set of hand-carved wooden figurines—a hobby her father had picked up during his quiet moments as a carpenter.

"Maybe..." Peyton whispered. A spark of hope ignited within her as she considered the possibility that the key to finding the cabin could be hidden among her parents' things. It was a long shot, but it was all she had.

It was Owen, a friend from her days at the FBI, who had generously offered her a free storage unit at his facility after hearing about her situation. At first, Peyton had been unsure about what to do with her parents' things while she worked on the cabin. She had even considered selling them. But eventually, she realized that she couldn't bear to part with them just yet, so she gratefully accepted Owen's offer.

Now, as she considered the possibility that the key to finding the cabin could be hidden among her parents' possessions, Peyton knew she had to act. Opening those boxes would be like ripping open an old wound, but it was a risk she was willing to take.

"Okay, let's do this," she said under her breath, determination filling her voice. She picked up her phone and dialed the number for Owen's storage facility.

"Thank you for calling Mountain View Storage," the recording chirped. "Our office hours are Tuesday through Friday, 9:00 a.m. to 5:00 p.m., and Saturday, 10:00 a.m. to 4:00 p.m. If you require assistance outside of these hours, please leave a message and we will return your call during our next business day."

"Damn," Peyton cursed quietly. Normally, she could access her unit around the clock thanks to the keypad on the front gate. However, Owen had mentioned during their last conversation that they were upgrading their security system, and the keypad was temporarily out of service.

"Of course it is," she said with a sigh, trying to quell her frustration. The sun was already creeping higher into the sky, casting brilliant rays of light through the windows. A new day had begun, but since today was Monday, Peyton would have to wait until tomorrow to continue her search for the truth.

"How am I going to pass the time?" she wondered aloud, her hands restlessly fidgeting with the phone. An entire day stretched out before her, and every hour felt like an eternity when weighed against the importance of her quest.

Then another idea occurred to her. Why not call Owen directly? Surely he would understand and offer to let her into her storage unit, even outside of business hours. She hated putting him to work on an off day, but this was important.

Peyton took a deep breath and dialed Owen's number, her heart pounding with anticipation. After a few rings, he answered with a groggy "Hello?"

"Owen, it's Peyton," she said, trying to keep the urgency out of her voice.

"Peyton? Is everything okay?" he asked, sounding more alert now.

"I need your help," she said, her voice shaking with emotion. "I know it's early and I'm sorry to bother you, but I need to get into my storage unit today."

"Is everything okay?" he repeated, concern evident in his voice.

"It's complicated," she said, struggling to keep her voice steady. "But I need to find something important and I can't wait until tomorrow."

There was a moment of silence on the other end of the line. Peyton held her breath, waiting for his response.

"I'm sorry, Peyton," he finally said. "I'm out of town, and I won't be back till late tonight."

She swallowed hard, trying to hold out hope. "Isn't there someone else who can let me in?"

"I'm afraid not," he replied. "I'm the only one with access to the security system right now."

Peyton felt a wave of disappointment wash over her. It seemed like every path she attempted to take was blocked by some obstacle.

She was about to ask another question, but just then she heard a woman's voice in the background.

"Sorry," Owen said to Peyton, "I've really gotta go. But come by first thing in the morning, alright?"

"Alright," she said softly, disappointed. "Thanks, Owen."

"No problem."

The phone went dead.

Peyton sat there for a few moments, staring at the phone screen with a defeated expression. She knew she had to wait until the next day to continue her search, but the urgency of her mission gnawed at her. She couldn't shake the feeling that there was something important waiting for her in that storage unit—something that could lead her to the elusive Red Pine Cabin.

Her thoughts were interrupted by the shrill ring of her phone. Her heart leaped, and for a moment she thought it might be Owen calling to say something had changed. But then she noticed the caller ID. It was Peter Marshal, her boss at the National Park Service.

A hardworking and dedicated man, Peter had always shown genuine concern for his employees, especially Peyton. She found him much easier to work for than her previous boss at the FBI.

"Hey, boss," she said, answering the call. "What's up?"

"Morning, Risk," Marshal replied, his voice warm and friendly. "I just wanted to check in on you. Have you had a chance to rest since wrapping up the last case? I know how much you put into your work, but remember, even the best rangers need some downtime."

"Thanks, Marshal," she replied, touched by his concern. "I've been taking it easy, but you know me—I'll be ready to dive back in soon enough."

"Actually," Marshal began hesitantly, "that's partly why I'm calling. There's something I'd like to discuss with you—a new case."

Peyton, sensing that there was more behind his words, furrowed her brow. "Why do I get the feeling you're not telling me everything?" she asked, only half-joking.

"Perceptive as always, Risk," Marshal responded, his tone suddenly serious. "This case is a bit unusual. It involves a pair of drownings in Great Smoky Mountains National Park."

"Tragic," Peyton said, her voice softening. "But what makes it unusual?"

"I need you to be extra careful on this one," Marshal warned, his words heavy with import.

"Why? What's going on?" Peyton asked, her heart rate quickening as the weight of his silence settled over her like a shroud.

"Because, Risk," he finally said, "one of the victims was a park ranger."

CHAPTER TWO

Peyton gazed out the small oval window of the plane, studying the rumpled ridges and valleys of the Smoky Mountains far below. The sight brought back a rush of memories from her childhood—hiking those trails, breathing the pine-scented air, roasting hot dogs and s'mores around the campfire. She could almost hear her dad's baritone voice and her mom's laughter echoing through the trees as she recalled one perfect summer trip when she was ten. They'd hiked to a waterfall, swimming in the crisp pool at its base. Peyton smiled faintly. If only she could go back to that carefree girl with her loving parents.

The drone of the engines shifted slightly as the plane began its descent. They should be landing soon at the small regional airport near the crime scene. She thought of the remote cabin her father once described that he'd used as a hideout during his outlaw days. It was somewhere in these mountains, long abandoned. What clues might it hold?

She felt Sean's eyes on her. "A penny for your thoughts?" he asked.

Peyton turned to him, considering for a moment. Sean had been so closed off when they first started working together, but over the past few cases, he'd slowly opened up. She decided to take a chance and be vulnerable with him in return.

"I was thinking about my parents," she admitted. "Remembering a trip we took here to the Smokies when I was a kid."

"Are you close with them?"

It occurred to Peyton that she hadn't ever told Sean about her parents' deaths. Now was as good a time as any. "I was," she began hesitantly. "But they died a long time ago."

Sean listened intently, his blue eyes softening with compassion. "I'm so sorry," he said. "What happened?"

She took a shaky breath. "I'm not sure. They were murdered, and I never learned who did it or why."

Sean's eyes widened in surprise. "Peyton, I had no idea. How come you never told me?"

Peyton shrugged. "It's not something I like to talk about. It's been so long, and I've just learned to live with the fact that I may never know what happened."

But the truth was, she hadn't learned to live with it. Not really. Every time she thought about her parents, it was like a raw wound had been reopened. She'd thrown herself into her work, becoming one of the best agents the FBI had, but despite the accolades and the successful cases, nothing could fill the void in her heart. She knew that, no matter how much she devoted herself to her new job with the NPS, no amount of success here would fill the void, either.

"After that," she continued, "I went into the foster system for a while."

"That must have been challenging," Sean said.

"Growing up in the foster system was difficult," Peyton admitted, her voice soft yet steady. "But it toughened me. It taught me to adapt quickly to new situations and to rely on myself."

"Can you give me an example?" Sean asked.

"Sure," she said, pausing for a moment to gather her thoughts. "I remember one winter when I was fourteen. My foster family at the time lived in a rundown house with poor insulation. The heating system broke down, and we had no money to fix it. I used my resourcefulness to find ways to stay warm—like layering old newspapers under my clothes and opening the oven door after baking, letting the heat escape into the living room." Peyton's eyes seemed to glaze over as she recalled the memory, but she shook off the melancholy and continued. "That experience taught me resilience and self-reliance."

Sean nodded. "Did you age out of the system, then?" he asked.

"No," replied Peyton, her expression brightening. "I was adopted by Saul Guzman when I was sixteen. He changed everything for me."

"Tell me more about him."

"Where do I start?" Peyton smiled warmly, her dark eyes lighting up at the mention of Saul. "Saul is a kind and patient man. He has this incredible ability to see potential in people that others might overlook. I was a troubled kid, but he believed in me and pushed me to find my own path."

"Sounds like a great guy," Sean said.

"Absolutely," Peyton agreed. "He's been a guiding force in my life, helping me to find my own strength and to trust my instincts. He encouraged me to join the FBI, and now, here I am, working with you."

Sean took a deep breath, as if gathering his thoughts. "I can relate to some of that. Growing up, my family moved around a lot due to my dad's job, so I never really had a chance to put down roots or form lasting friendships. It was tough, but it taught me to be self-sufficient."

Peyton listened attentively, her eyes fixed on Sean as he shared more of his life's story. She noticed the vulnerability in his voice and realized that this was probably not something he talked about often.

"Eventually, we settled in Montana," Sean continued. "That's where I fell in love with the outdoors and found solace in wilderness survival. It became my passion, and when I started working for the NPS, it felt like I'd finally found my purpose."

As Sean finished speaking, Peyton reflected on how aloof he had been when they first met. With his guarded demeanor and lingering grief over his previous partner, Gabriela Esposito, she had initially doubted their ability to work together effectively. However, as they spent more time together, slowly breaking through each other's barriers, Peyton found herself respecting Sean and even growing to enjoy working with him.

"Thank you for sharing that, Sean," she said, genuinely touched by his openness. "I think it's amazing that we've both managed to find our way here, despite the challenges we've faced."

"Life has a funny way of turning out sometimes," Sean agreed, a hint of a smile appearing on his lean, angular face.

An easy silence settled between them for a few moments.

"Well, enough about me," she said with a wave of her hand. "We'd better go over the case file."

Sean's gaze lingered on her for a few moments longer, studying her. Then he nodded and stooped to pick up the file from where it was lying on his duffel bag.

As Sean flipped through the case file, Peyton studied him. It was hard to believe this was the same aloof, standoffish man she'd first met weeks ago. Back then, Sean had kept her at arm's length, clearly reluctant to work with a new partner. But gradually, his frostiness had thawed.

Now they'd settled into an easy camaraderie. Sean's dry humor and steadfast competence had won her over. She respected his knowledge and skills in the wilderness. And she had to admit, his angular features and piercing blue eyes weren't exactly hard on the eyes, either.

A smile played on Peyton's lips. Who would've thought she'd actually grow to like the stubborn Montana mountain man? But she was glad to call him partner. Together, they made a good team.

Sean glanced up, catching her gaze. "What are you grinning about?"

"Oh, nothing,"Peyton said lightly. "Just thinking we've come a long way from those first few frigid weeks of working together."

"Still holding that against me?"

She shrugged one shoulder coyly. "A little."

He playfully shoved the file into her hands. "Why don't you read up? Maybe it'll keep you out of trouble."

She rolled her eyes. Then, sighing, she opened the file, her eyes scanning the pages inside, absorbing every detail. According to the file, two women had been found drowned in the park—one two months ago named Kimberly Saunders, a local teacher, and the other just this morning, a park ranger named Amanda Torres.

"It's a little troubling, knowing the killer targeted a park ranger," she said.

Sean nodded. "It definitely raises the stakes. Not to mention, it suggests the killer may have some knowledge of the park and the people who work here."

Peyton's eyes narrowed as she looked over the file. "There's also the fact that both victims were women who were alone at the time."

Sean leaned in closer, his rugged features etched with concern. "What does that tell you?"

Peyton paused to gather her thoughts before speaking. "It could suggest that the killer targets vulnerable women who are alone and isolated. It's possible that he's using the park as a hunting ground."

Sean's jaw clenched at the thought. "We need to find this guy fast before he strikes again."

Peyton nodded. "The file mentions that the bodies were found near the river. Do you think there could be any significance to that?"

"It's possible," Sean said, rubbing his chin thoughtfully. "The river spans miles across the park, so it's a vast area to search. But it's a start."

Peyton flipped through the file, looking for any other clues that might help them. As she scanned the pages, her eyes fell on something written about the first victim, Kimberly Saunders. Though she'd been an elementary school teacher at the time of her death, her previous occupation had been as a police officer.

A chill ran down Peyton's spine as she considered the implications.

"Maybe that's the connection," she murmured. "Both victims were involved in some form of law enforcement. That could be why the killer picked them."

"And if you're right," Sean said slowly, "we'll have to be careful. Because he might just pick us next."

CHAPTER THREE

"Feels like we're in the middle of nowhere," Peyton remarked, taking in the remote surroundings as she and Sean hiked through the forest along the dirt path. The scent of damp earth and fallen leaves filled her nostrils, while the rustling of branches overhead created a natural symphony, punctuated by the occasional chirp of a bird or the hum of an insect.

The towering trees – maples, oaks, and hickories – formed a dense canopy above them, filtering sunlight that dappled their path with shifting patterns of light and shadow. Patches of rhododendrons and mountain laurel lined the trail, their evergreen leaves providing a stark contrast to the barren branches around them. It was troubling for Peyton to imagine someone being attacked out here, so far from civilization.

"Seems that way," Sean agreed, his eyes scanning the area as they walked.

Peyton nodded, glancing at the small flags tied to branches along the way, marking their path. She couldn't help but think about the recording she'd listened to earlier that morning—her father's voice, filled with fear and urgency, speaking of the mysterious Red Pine Cabin. She longed to access the storage unit containing her parents' belongings, to search for any clue that might lead her to the cabin. But for now, she had no choice but to focus on the case at hand.

"Is it much farther?" Peyton asked, brushing aside a low-hanging branch as they continued along the trail.

Sean paused suddenly, cocking his head. "Did you hear that?" he asked.

Peyton stopped and listened intently. At first, she couldn't discern what he was referring to, but then she picked up on it—the sound of rushing water growing louder as they moved forward.

"We must be getting close to the river," she said.

"Ember River," Sean said with a hint of fondness.

"You're familiar with it?"

"Sure am. It starts at Ember Lake, which is how the river got its name. When the sun sets over the water, it casts a shimmering glow like burning embers."

"Sounds beautiful."

He nodded. "It is. From there, the river stretches for about seventy miles, winding through the park and eventually merging with another larger river."

"Wow, you know a lot about this place," Peyton said, genuinely impressed by Sean's knowledge of the area.

"I've been here quite a few times over the years," he replied, a hint of pride in his voice. "The wilderness has always been a big part of my life, just like yours."

Hearing him mention her connection to the outdoors brought a bittersweet pang to Peyton's chest. The beauty of the Great Smoky Mountains reminded her of her time spent exploring Eden's Gate National Park with her parents, moments now tainted by the unsolved mystery surrounding their deaths.

The sound of rushing water grew louder, and as Peyton and Sean broke through the tree line, they finally laid eyes on the river. The Ember River cut through the landscape like a serpentine ribbon, its clear waters churning with power and purpose. Sunlight cast dappled patterns onto the river's surface, causing the water to sparkle like a cascade of diamonds.

"Quite a sight," Peyton murmured, taking in the breathtaking view before her eyes scanned the area, searching for any sign of the rangers they were supposed to meet.

A short distance away, a group of park rangers stood on the bank, their expressions somber and shoulders slumped. They talked among themselves in hushed tones, their pain evident even from afar. It was clear they were hurting from the loss of Amanda Torres, one of their own.

As Peyton and Sean approached the group, one of the rangers noticed them and broke away from his colleagues. He was a tall man with a muscular build that suggested a life spent working outdoors. His sandy brown hair was cropped short, and he had a neatly trimmed beard framing a strong jawline. Lines around his eyes hinted at countless hours squinting against the sun, and his deep green eyes seemed to hold a reservoir of unshed tears.

"I'm Ranger Ian Glass," he said, extending a calloused hand to both Peyton and Sean. "You must be the agents from the National Park Service."

"Peyton Risk and Sean O'Malley," Peyton said, shaking his hand firmly. "We're here to investigate Amanda Torres's death."

"Of course." Ranger Glass nodded, his voice heavy with sorrow. "Her body was discovered early this morning by one of our maintenance workers near the edge of the water. Other than pulling her out of the water, we haven't touched anything since we found her—we've been waiting for you to arrive."

"Thank you, Ranger Glass. We appreciate your cooperation," Sean said. "We'll do our best to find out what happened."

"Please, call me Ian," he said, a flicker of gratitude in his eyes. "If there's anything we can do to help, don't be afraid to ask."

Peyton hesitated for a moment, taking in Ian Glass's somber expression before asking, "Did you know Amanda well?"

Ian's eyes met her gaze steadily, though the pain within them was unmistakable. "Yes, I did," he replied quietly. "Amanda and I worked together on a number of projects in the park. She had a passion for preserving the environment and helping others appreciate its beauty."

"Sounds like she was a dedicated ranger," Peyton observed, hoping to encourage Ian to share more about Amanda.

"Very much so," Ian agreed, his voice heavy with emotion. "She was always eager to learn and improve her skills, and her enthusiasm was contagious. It's hard to believe someone like her could be gone so suddenly."

As Ian spoke, another ranger called out to him from across the riverbank. "Ian, we need you over here!"

"Excuse me," Ian said, his professional demeanor reasserting itself as he turned to address the other ranger. "I'll be right there."

Peyton nodded, watching Ian walk away before turning to Sean. "We should go see the body," she suggested.

Sean gave her a solemn nod of agreement, and together they carefully picked their way along the bank toward the spot where Amanda Torres's lifeless form lay partially covered by a tarp.

Despite her years of experience in dealing with crime scenes and the tragic aftermaths of violence, Peyton couldn't help but feel a knot of unease tightening in her stomach. The sight of a dead body never became routine, and each victim carried with them a reminder of the fragility of life—especially when that victim was young and full of potential, like Amanda.

As they approached, the murmur of the river seemed to grow louder, mixing with the sounds of the forest and the subdued voices of the rangers nearby. The air was cool, but not uncomfortably so, and the scent of damp earth and fallen leaves filled Peyton's nostrils. She and Sean walked with purpose, their footsteps causing the occasional crunch of foliage underfoot.

As they neared the spot, Peyton caught sight of Amanda's lifeless form lying on the bank, partially concealed by a tarp. She was wearing her ranger uniform, the green fabric now stained and disheveled from her time in the water. Amanda's once vibrant face was pale and lifeless, a haunting reminder of the tragedy that had occurred.

As they got closer, Peyton noticed signs that Amanda's body had been submerged for a while; her skin appeared swollen and discolored, with visible signs of decomposition starting to set in. A mixture of sadness and determination washed over her as she steeled herself for the grim task ahead.

Sean, his expression stoic but his eyes betraying a hint of sorrow, stood beside Peyton as they observed the body. He took a deep breath before saying, "It's never easy, is it?"

"No," Peyton admitted quietly. "But we have a job to do."

Taking one last look at Amanda's lifeless form, Peyton knelt beside the body and began examining it more closely. She looked for any self-defense wounds or other signs of struggle. She discovered a few faint bruises on Amanda's arm.

Did someone grab her? Peyton wondered. She couldn't quite tell. It was equally possible Amanda had received the bruises more innocently.Meanwhile, Sean surveyed the area around them, searching for any clues or signs that could help piece together the events leading up to Amanda's death. Peyton glanced up at him and asked, "What are you thinking?"

Sean furrowed his brow, deep in thought. "I don't think her body traveled far downstream," he said finally.

"Really? Why do you say that?"

He pointed upstream to some large rocks and a fallen tree partially submerged in the river. "See those obstacles? If her body had come from farther up, it would've likely been caught on one of those. It seems more likely that she drowned here, in this area."

Peyton's gaze shifted from Amanda's lifeless body to the surroundings. As she scanned the opposite bank of the river, she spotted a rocky overlook jutting out over the water. The cliff face was rugged and uneven, covered in patches of moss and lichen, while the dense foliage provided a natural barrier around the edges.

"Hey, Sean," she said, pointing at the rocky formation. "What if Amanda fell from there?"

He nodded, his eyes narrowing as he studied the overlook. "Yes, that's definitely possible." His tone suggested he was holding something back.

"What is it?" Peyton asked.

"Do you really think she fell? Or was she pushed?"

CHAPTER FOUR

There's got to be a shallow place where we can cross this river, Peyton thought as she and Sean marched along its bank, searching for a way to get to the bluff.

The Ember River, true to its name, sparkled like molten gold under the morning sun. Its waters were clear and fast-moving, revealing a rocky bed scattered with fallen leaves and branches. On either side, the forest loomed tall and silent, a tapestry of greens and browns that muffled even the faintest sounds.

The terrain was challenging, with the ground often giving way to slippery mud or tangled roots that threatened to trip them up. Despite this, Peyton couldn't help but feel invigorated by the wild beauty of the park. It reminded her of the countless trips she'd taken with her parents, exploring nature's hidden secrets together. She wished they were here now, helping her unravel the mystery of Amanda Torres's death.

"Here," Sean said, pointing to a spot where the river narrowed, and a series of large, flat boulders spanned the gap between the two banks. "This should be easier to cross."

"Lead the way," Peyton replied, watching as Sean expertly hopped from one rock to another, maintaining his balance with the grace of a seasoned outdoorsman.

Taking a deep breath, she followed him, stepping carefully onto the first boulder, feeling the slick surface beneath her boots. As she reached for the next rock, her foot slipped, sending her heart racing as she teetered on the edge of the rushing water. But before she could fall in, Sean's hand shot out, gripping her arm firmly and pulling her back to safety.

"Thanks," she muttered, cheeks flushed with embarrassment as she steadied herself and continued to make her way across the remaining rocks.

"Any time," Sean replied with a grin, his eyes gleaming with a mix of relief and amusement.

Once safely on the other side, they faced the challenge of climbing a steep slope covered in thick underbrush. The uneven terrain was difficult to navigate, and they had to push through tangled webs of branches and vines that seemed to reach out, stubbornly clinging to their clothing and gear.

"Are you sure you don't want to turn back?" Sean teased, wiping beads of sweat from his brow as he plunged ahead, creating a path for Peyton to follow. "I won't blame you if you do."

"Nice try," Peyton shot back, her competitive nature kicking in. "But I wouldn't want you to get lonely out here, all by yourself in the big bad forest."

He snorted in reply as they continued their ascent, each step bringing them closer to the rocky overlook where Amanda Torres may have met her tragic end.

Suddenly, they broke through the brush and found themselves standing on the rocky outcropping they had spotted from below. A breathtaking view of the river stretched out before them; it twisted and turned like a silver ribbon, its surface sparkling in the early morning light. The vibrant green foliage of the surrounding forest seemed to embrace the water, creating a picturesque scene that was both serene and awe-inspiring.

"Wow," Peyton said, momentarily forgetting their grim purpose for being there. "This is absolutely beautiful."

"Definitely worth the climb," Sean agreed, his eyes taking in the scenery with equal appreciation.

As they stood there, the tranquility of the moment allowed Peyton to feel a fleeting sense of connection with the natural world. But the peace was short-lived, as Peyton's gaze fell upon muddy footprints near the edge of the cliff. She stooped down to study the tracks more closely. There were several distinct prints, some larger than others, pressed into the soft earth. The edges were slightly blurred, suggesting that they had been made recently before the ground had fully dried after last night's rain.

"We should get a team out here to cast these prints," she said. "Some might belong to the killer."

Sean crouched beside her, examining the tracks as well. "It doesn't look like there was much of a struggle," he said.

"How are you so sure?" Peyton asked.

"See how the footprints are spaced evenly and consistently?" Sean explained. "If there had been a struggle, we'd likely see scuff marks or signs of someone being dragged. These prints suggest that whoever was here walked calmly to the edge, without any resistance."

Peyton frowned—she could have figured that much out on her own. Still, she appreciated the insight.

The lack of struggle hinted at a more complex scenario than a simple attack, but what could have led Amanda Torres to this remote location with her potential killer?

"Maybe the killer forced Amanda to jump," she mused, her eyes still fixed on the muddy footprints. "He could've threatened her with a knife or a gun, or used some other kind of incentive."

Sean gazed down at the winding river below. "Maybe. But that doesn't explain what killed her."

"What do you mean?"

"A fall from this height probably wouldn't be fatal," he pointed out. "The water below is deep, without any prominent rocks. Besides, a ranger would know how to swim. So, how did Amanda drown?"

Peyton chewed on her lower lip, considering the possibilities. Something about Sean's observation nagged at her, but she couldn't quite put her finger on it. As they stood in silence, the distant sound of birdsong filled the air, further emphasizing the eerie incongruity of the peaceful scene before them and the violent death that had occurred here.

While pondering this, Peyton's keen eye caught something unusual: vehicle tracks nearby. She crouched down to study them more closely. They appeared to be from a golf cart. The tire marks were fresh, cutting deep into the soft earth and creating an easily traceable path.

"Sean, look at these tracks," she called, gesturing for him to join her. "They're from a golf cart. They lead away along the edge of the cliff, where there's a dirt road." She glanced up at him, her brow furrowed. "Do you think the killer might have used the cart to transport Amanda here?"

Sean's eyes narrowed as he studied the tracks. "I don't know," he said quietly, a grim expression settling on his face. "But I think we'd better follow them and find out."

CHAPTER FIVE

Arnold trudged through the damp forest, his shoes squelching with every step. Cold droplets of water clung to the leaves above, remnants of last night's rain. The air was thick with the earthy scent of decaying leaves and moist soil.

As Arnold walked, his mind flashed back to his struggle with the ranger, replaying the scene like a twisted movie. He recalled the adrenaline coursing through his veins as he leaped from the bluff into the churning waters of the river below, the satisfaction that had washed over him as he grabbed her just as she was about to escape the river's grasp. He remembered wrestling with her in the cold water, his limbs coiled around her like an alligator, pulling her down and down until her body finally went limp.

"Too easy," Arnold muttered under his breath, his pleasure at the memory quickly wilting into disappointment. He had always placed people in law enforcement on a pedestal, believing them to be infallible and untouchable. The woman, being a ranger, should have been more difficult to overpower. But now, Arnold knew the truth—they were just as flawed, just as vulnerable as anyone else. And it was this realization that filled him with a perverse sense of power.

"Maybe they're not so special after all," he mused, thinking back to his childhood when he'd watch cop shows on TV with wide-eyed wonder. The heroes always caught the bad guys, thwarting their sinister plans with ease. But reality was far different from fiction. If anything, his encounter with the ranger only served to prove how easily these so-called protectors could be brought down by someone like him.

As Arnold trudged on, the damp earth clinging to his shoes with each step, he found himself thinking about how his father had once urged him to join the military. His father had believed that the structure and discipline of the armed forces would mold Arnold into a better man, one who could contribute positively to society. But Arnold knew back then that the military life wasn't for him—he couldn't stomach the thought of following orders from superiors without questioning their motives.

Instead, Arnold had chosen a different path, one that took him further away from the expectations his father had imposed upon him. He drifted from job to job, finding satisfaction in none of them, ultimately discovering a dark hunger within himself. This twisted desire to test others' weaknesses became the driving force in his life, giving him purpose where the military never could have.

"Excuse me, sir?" a voice interrupted his thoughts. Startled, Arnold's pulse quickened as he looked up to see a young ranger only a few paces away. The ranger appeared inexperienced, with a clean-shaven face and eyes that conveyed a sense of naivety. Despite his youthful appearance, the ranger was armed with a holstered handgun at his side.

Arnold's heart raced as he weighed his options, his mind swirling with thoughts of how to handle the situation. If the ranger knew who he was, then Arnold needed to silence him before he could call for reinforcements. He watched the young ranger intently, analyzing his movements and searching for any sign of recognition or suspicion in his eyes. As Arnold clenched his fists, he formulated a plan for a swift and silent takedown.

"Are you alone, sir?" the ranger asked.

"Yes."

The ranger studied Arnold, and Arnold had the impression that he ought to introduce himself. "Guy," he said, going with the first name that came to mind. "Call me Guy."

"Alright, Guy," the ranger said slowly, as if still evaluating him. "Have you been to the Ember River today, by any chance?"

"No," Arnold lied, his voice calm despite the adrenaline surging through his veins. Then it hit him—he was soaking wet. His shoes squelched with every step, and his clothes clung to his body like a second skin. He braced himself for the ranger to call him out on the lie, but the ranger seemed oblivious to his damp attire.

"Is everything okay?" the ranger continued, his eyes darting around the wooded area as if expecting danger to materialize from the shadows. "What were you doing out here?"

Arnold paused for a moment, his mind racing to concoct a plausible story. "I was... birdwatching," he said, feigning enthusiasm. "I'm an amateur ornithologist, you see. I've been following a rare species of woodpecker that's been spotted in these parts—the ivory-billed woodpecker. Thought I might catch a glimpse."

"Ah, I see," the ranger replied, nodding as if he found the explanation satisfactory. Arnold fought back a smirk, marveling at the ranger's gullibility. "Did you see one?"

"See what?"

"An ivory-billed woodpecker."

"Unfortunately not." Arnold sighed, playing along with the charade. "But I'll keep looking. You never know when something might turn up."

"True," the ranger agreed, though it was clear his mind was elsewhere.

He's going to notice my clothes, Arnold thought, his fear growing. *He'll realize I was in the river, and then he'll–*

Suddenly, the ranger's radio crackled to life, and a garbled voice came through the speaker. The ranger turned away from Arnold and spoke into the radio in a low, hushed tone. This was Arnold's chance. With the ranger distracted, he could sneak up behind him and strike.

His muscles tensed, Arnold crept closer to the unsuspecting ranger. The ground beneath his feet was damp and littered with fallen leaves, but he moved with surprising stealth. As he closed the distance between them, he spotted a sizable rock on the ground. It would be perfect for knocking the ranger out cold.

Just as Arnold stooped to pick up the rock, the ranger finished his conversation and abruptly turned around. Thinking fast, Arnold pretended he was merely tying his boot. The ranger eyed him for a moment before shaking his head sadly.

"Such a tragedy—someone fell into the river and drowned yesterday," the ranger said, his expression somber.

"Really?" Arnold feigned surprise. "Was it a suicide?"

"We're not sure yet," the ranger admitted. "It could have been. We're still investigating."

A smirk tugged at the corner of Arnold's mouth as he realized the rangers were none the wiser about the true nature of the woman's death. He felt a surge of power coursing through him, bolstering his confidence that he'd get away with the killing.

"Anyway," the ranger said with a sigh, "I need to go. We're short-staffed, and there's still a lot of ground to cover." His eyes met Arnold's, and he offered a polite smile. "Take care and enjoy your hike, Guy."

"Thanks," Arnold replied, feigning gratitude. As the ranger turned and walked away, Arnold couldn't help but shake his head in disbelief at his good fortune. He'd narrowly evaded capture, and the authorities were none the wiser.

With renewed determination, Arnold continued on, hurrying deeper into the woods. The sun filtered through the dense canopy overhead, casting dappled light across the forest floor. The air was heavy with the scent of damp earth and decaying leaves, while the distant melody of a songbird punctuated the otherwise quiet morning.

Arnold's thoughts wandered, more convinced than ever that fate was on his side. This was just the beginning—other people needed to be tested, just like he had tested Amanda and Kimberly. And he was more than happy to administer those tests.

As he forged further into the shadowy depths of the park, Arnold began to plot his next move. Unbeknownst to the people who crossed his path, they would soon be pawns in his twisted game. And for Arnold, there was no greater thrill than holding their lives in the palm of his hand.

CHAPTER SIX

"If we were smart," Peyton said, rubbing her arms to ward off the morning chill, "we would've brought ATVs."

She studied the dirt path ahead of her as it cut through the forest like a jagged scar. The trail was narrow and uneven, littered with rocks and roots that snaked their way across the ground, daring them to trip.

Peyton and Sean had been following this trail for over an hour now, their boots crunching on the damp earth, muscles aching from the constant uphill climb. There was no telling how much longer they'd have to follow it, but the determined set of Sean's jaw told Peyton he wasn't about to give up any time soon. The golf cart tracks were their only lead, and Peyton was hopeful the tracks would tell them something – anything – about the killer.

"Think we should turn back?" Sean asked. "We've been at this for a while."

Peyton considered, her gaze drifting back to the trail before them, where it disappeared into the dense underbrush. She sighed. "It wouldn't hurt to call for someone to drive out to meet us. That way, if we need to go all the way back, we won't have to waste our time walking." She hated the idea of admitting defeat, especially after all the progress they've made, but she knew pragmatism was key in cases like these.

Sean nodded and pulled out his phone, scrolling through his contacts.

"Who are you calling?" Peyton asked.

"I've got a friend who works here." He paused as the phone rang. "Hey, Jesse," he said a moment later, it's Sean. Listen, we could use some help out here. We're following a dirt road away from the Ember River, and it's taking us deeper into the woods than we anticipated. Could you meet us with an RTV or something?"

As Sean spoke quietly into his phone, Peyton took the opportunity to study the surrounding area in greater detail. The dirt path they'd been following for over an hour was uneven and narrow, flanked on either side by tall trees whose branches stretched out like skeletal fingers. The forest floor was a patchwork of decaying leaves and foliage, releasing a damp, earthy scent that mingled with the crisp morning air.

Her mind wandered back to the image of Amanda's lifeless body on the bank of the river, her once-vibrant essence snuffed out by the cold, unforgiving waters. Had she been alive when she was placed in that golf cart? Or had she already met her end by that point, her body a mere shell as the murderer sought to dispose of the evidence?

The nagging questions gnawed at her, demanding answers that she didn't yet possess. Where was the golf cart now? Had the killer managed to dispose of it without leaving a trace, or was it still hidden somewhere in the depths of the park, a vital clue waiting to be unearthed?

"Jesse's on his way," Sean said, snapping Peyton from her thoughts. "He should be here with an RTV in about ten minutes."

"Great," Peyton replied, relieved that they wouldn't have to trek back through the woods on foot if this lead turned out to be a dead end. As they continued along, she decided to delve further into Sean's connection with their soon-to-arrive ally. "So, how did you meet Jesse?"

"During a search and rescue mission a few years ago," Sean explained, gazing into the distance as if the memories lay just beyond the trees. "He's a park ranger, been working here for quite some time. Solid guy, knows the area like the back of his hand."

Peyton nodded, appreciating the insight into Sean's past. It had been a slow process, but she felt like she was finally getting to know Sean better—understanding the man behind the stoic wilderness survival specialist facade. With each passing day, she grew more comfortable in their partnership, and she couldn't help but hope that Sean felt the same.

The forest began to awaken around them—birds singing high above, insects buzzing through the underbrush, and the distant rustle of what she assumed to be small animals scurrying about. Then, without warning, the forest broke and they were standing at the edge of an expansive golf course, its rolling hills and manicured greens a vibrant contrast to the untamed wilderness they'd been navigating for over an hour. The dew-kissed grass glistened in the sunlight, and a light mist clung to the earth like a ghostly shroud.

"Finally," Peyton muttered, her muscles aching from traversing the rough terrain. She glanced at Sean, who surveyed the golf course with furrowed brows, his disappointment evident.

"Unfortunately, tracking the golf cart won't be possible here," he said, running a hand through his short-cropped hair. "There are too many tracks, and the turf makes it difficult to determine which ones are fresh."

Peyton sighed, frustration gnawing at her insides. They'd been so close, following the trail left by the mysterious golf cart that might have been used by Amanda's killer. Now, it seemed their lead had evaporated before their eyes.

As she scanned the empty golf course, pondering their next move, a distant hum caught her attention. Squinting against the brightness of the morning sun, she spotted a golf cart approaching across the vast expanse of green. It was a small, white vehicle, with knobby tires and a canvas roof, bouncing recklessly over the undulating landscape.

"Looks like Jesse's here," Sean said, shading his eyes with his hand.

As the golf cart drew nearer, Peyton could see the driver more clearly—a tall, broad-shouldered man in his early forties, with sandy blond hair and rugged features. He waved energetically as he approached, a friendly grin splitting his wind-chapped face.

"Hey there!" he called out, bringing the cart to a halt beside Peyton and Sean. "You folks need a lift?"

"Good to see you, man," Sean said, shaking his friend's hand before gesturing toward Peyton. "This is Peyton Risk, my partner on this case."

"Nice to meet you, Peyton," Jesse said, extending his hand to her.

"Likewise," she replied, returning the firm handshake.

"Thanks for coming out here so quickly," Sean said.

Jesse smiled again. "No problem. Hop on in."

Peyton hesitated. "Before we do that, would you mind taking a look at the tracks here in the woods? We're trying to figure out which vehicle might have made them."

Jesse climbed out of his cart and joined Peyton and Sean at the edge of the woods. He furrowed his brow as he studied the tracks, squatting down for a closer inspection. After a few moments, he shook his head. "There's no way to be certain," he admitted. "These tracks are too faint, and there are so many golf carts around here that it'd be impossible to identify one set specifically."

Peyton sighed in frustration, her gaze following the dirt road that led from the golf course, disappearing into the dense forest beyond. "Why is there even a path leading out from the golf course to the river?" she asked.

Jesse straightened up and brushed off his hands. "It's a fire access road. It allows emergency vehicles to reach more remote areas of the park quickly if needed."

"Does anyone ever drive along that road using a golf cart?" Sean asked. "Not to put out a fire, I mean?"

Jesse considered the question for a moment before answering. "Well, sometimes the golf course manager, Lenny Furtich, rides out along the trail. He calls it his 'me time,' says he needs mental space now and then."

That caught Peyton's attention. "Did Lenny know Amanda Torres, by any chance?" she asked.

Jesse's face clouded. He shifted uncomfortably under her gaze, glancing at Sean before responding. "I don't really know how much I should share."

Sean placed a reassuring hand on Jesse's shoulder. "It's okay, you can be honest with us. We're trying to find out what happened to Amanda."

"Alright." Jesse sighed, seeming to relax slightly. "I've never heard Lenny talk about her...but there's a rumor that suggests he did know her."

"A rumor?" Peyton asked.

Jesse nodded, pressing his lips together tightly. "According to the grapevine, they were dating—and not only that, but they kept it very hush-hush, too. Didn't even tell friends and family. The only reason anyone knows about it is because one of Lenny's employees spotted them together."

"Why did they care if others knew?" Peyton asked.

Jesse shook his head. "Who knows? But considering the lengths they went to in order to keep the matter quiet…I'd say it must've been a pretty big secret."

CHAPTER SEVEN

Doesn't seem to have much weighing on his mind, Peyton thought, studying Lenny Furtich as he lectured one of his teenage employees on the importance of keeping the golf course clean.

As she and Sean waited for the right moment to approach Lenny, Peyton took in her surroundings. The golf course spread out before her like a lush green carpet, dotted with sand traps and water hazards that shimmered under the weak winter sun. In the distance, she could see the driving range, where a lone golfer practiced his swing with steady determination. The trees surrounding the course were mostly bare now.

"The condition of this course reflects on all of us," Lenny was saying to his employee, a scrawny youth who stooped in front of his boss as if expecting a slap at any moment. "If it looks perfect, people will think *we're* perfect. If it looks sloppy, they'll think *we're* sloppy. And that affects business."

He paused and looked the teenager up and down with a critical eye, as if assessing whether the boy was capable of maintaining the high standards Lenny demanded. "So never let your guard down," he continued. "Even the smallest detail can make a difference. Understand?"

The teenager nodded, swallowing hard, clearly intimidated by Lenny's air of superiority. Peyton noticed that Lenny seemed to take pleasure in asserting his authority, making sure everyone knew who was in charge.

It was then that Lenny finally noticed Peyton and Sean standing nearby, watching the interaction. He appeared puzzled for a moment, as though trying to determine why they were there. Then, with a slight nod to the teenager, he dismissed him. "You can go now. Just remember what I've told you."

"Y-yes, sir," the teenager stammered, and hurried off to resume his work.

Lenny approached Peyton and Sean, his expression shifting from one of puzzlement to mild curiosity. "Can I help you?" he asked, his tone guarded.

"Mr. Furtich," Peyton said, "I'm Peyton Risk, and this is my partner, Sean O'Malley. We're with the National Park Service."

Lenny's eyes narrowed slightly as he processed the information. "Is there something I can help you with?"

Sean made a show of looking around, clearly impressed with the golf course. "I've gotta say, this is quite a place you've got here. How long have you been working here?"

"I've been the manager for about twelve years now," Lenny said, puffing out his chest with pride. "Started out as a groundskeeper, then moved up to assistant manager before taking over the top position."

As Lenny spoke, Peyton couldn't help but notice the way he carried himself—tall, confident, and clearly proud of his accomplishments. His hands were calloused from years of hard work on the golf course, and his suntanned face bore the lines of someone who had spent countless hours outdoors.

Peyton decided to cut to the chase. "Do you know someone by the name of Amanda Torres?"

For a moment, Lenny hesitated, looking uncomfortable. Then, cautiously, he said, "Yes, I believe she's one of the rangers here at the park. Why do you ask?"

"Amanda was found dead in the Ember River earlier today. We're trying to piece together what happened to her."

At this revelation, Lenny's face paled, and his eyes widened in shock. He took a step back, his expression a mixture of disbelief and sorrow. "Oh, my God," he whispered, covering his mouth with one hand. "How...how is that possible? Did someone hurt her?"

"That's what we're trying to figure out," Peyton said, studying him closely. It seemed clear to her that he did indeed know Amanda, and that her death had come as a complete surprise to him. She didn't want to make any assumptions, however.

Lenny shook his head, still in disbelief. His eyes took on a glazed expression, as if he was struggling to comprehend the reality of what had happened. "Amanda was a good ranger," he said finally, his voice rough with emotion. "She cared about the park and the people who came here. I...I can't believe she's gone." There was a rawness in his voice that suggested the loss affected him personally in a way he was not admitting.

"How well did you know her?" Peyton asked.

Lenny ran a trembling hand over his face and swallowed hard. "Not very well, to be honest."

Peyton and Sean exchanged a glance.

"You sure about that?" Peyton asked. "You seem pretty shaken up."

"How could I not be?"

"We were told you knew her pretty well," Sean said.

Lenny looked startled. "What are you talking about?"

"This will go better for you," Sean said, "if you're honest. Lying about a potential murder victim isn't a good look."

Lenny licked his lips nervously. "You think she was murdered?"

Neither Peyton nor Sean said anything. Peyton decided it was better just to let him sweat.

Lenny looked away, his face clouding. Then he sighed. "Okay, okay. I only lied because—well, I'll get to that later. But yes, I knew her. Amanda and I, we were...involved. Romantically, I mean. But we kept it a secret, didn't tell anyone."

"Why'd you keep it a secret?" Peyton asked.

"Because of her ex-boyfriend," Lenny said, a hint of bitterness in his voice as he turned back to face her. "He was bad news, and Amanda didn't want him finding out about us. She was afraid he'd cause trouble for both of us."

"Trouble?"

Lenny shrugged. "Who knows? He's something of a wild card."

"When did you last see Amanda?" Sean asked.

"Two nights ago," Lenny said, his expression turning somber. "We met up after work, went for a walk along the river, and had dinner at a little diner not far from here. Everything seemed...normal. She was happy, laughing, telling me about her plans for the future."

"She didn't express any worries, any concerns?" Peyton asked, trying to piece together Amanda's state of mind before her death.

"No, none at all," Lenny insisted. "She was just...Amanda. Full of life and energy, always looking forward to what came next." He swallowed hard again, as if tears were threatening to well up.

Peyton studied Lenny's face, searching for any signs of deceit. "Where were you early this morning?"

Lenny didn't hesitate. "I start work at five every morning. There are plenty of people who can vouch for me—other employees, even some of the early-bird golfers. I've been on the job since before dawn, tending to the course and making sure everything is in order."

"Let's go back to the ex-boyfriend," Sean said. "Tell us a little more about him."

Lenny nodded, his jaw clenching in frustration. "Grady Jenkins. He's part of a biker gang around these parts. The guy is a real jerk—I can't stand him because of what he did to Amanda." His fingers curled into fists at his sides, knuckles turning white with the effort of containing his rage.

"What exactly did Grady do to Amanda?" Peyton asked.

Lenny's eyes flashed with anger as he recounted the details. "Amanda told me she was abused by Grady during their relationship. He was controlling, manipulative, and violent. She showed me bruises he'd left on her, and she told me stories about how he'd belittle her in front of his friends." As he spoke, it was clear that Lenny was struggling to hold back his emotions, his voice growing strained.

It made sense now. Lenny and Amanda had kept their relationship a secret for fear of what Grady might do. Had he found out and retaliated? If so, might Lenny be next?

She decided to see if she could connect Lenny to the previous victim.

"Kimberly Saunders," she said, shifting gears in the conversation. "Do you know anything about her?"

Lenny furrowed his brow, clearly trying to place the name. "Saunders? I'm not familiar with her. Who is she?"

"Two months ago, she drowned in the Ember River," Sean said.

Recognition flickered in Lenny's eyes, and he nodded. "Ah, yes, I remember hearing about that. Terrible thing. It was a suicide, wasn't it?"

"Unclear at this point," Peyton replied. She studied Lenny, noting the creases of concern on his forehead. "You sure you didn't know her?"

He pressed his lips together in a thin, humorless smile. "If you're asking whether I was secretly dating her, I assure you I was not."

"Just checking."

"Where can we find Grady Jenkins?" Sean asked.

Lenny hesitated for a moment, then pointed toward the edge of the park. "There's a biker bar on the outskirts. The Rusty Sprocket. He might be there. That's where he and his gang usually hang out."

"Thank you," Sean said. "We appreciate your help."

Lenny nodded, his eyes taking on a far-off look again—contemplating Amanda's death, no doubt. It would take a long time for the implications of the loss to set in.

As Peyton and Sean turned to leave, Lenny's voice stopped them. "Hey, be careful, alright?"

Peyton looked back at him, curious. "Why?"

"Because that bar has a nasty reputation. Fights break out all the time, and some of them end with people being hauled off on stretchers." Lenny's expression darkened. "And if Grady's there with his gang, he'll be more than ready for a fight."

CHAPTER EIGHT

Peyton silently counted the motorcycles lined up outside the Rusty Sprocket. The collection of chrome and steel gleamed under the morning sun, their bulky frames casting long shadows across the gravel parking lot. Some bikes bore custom paint jobs; others were adorned with leather saddlebags and intricate detailing on their gas tanks.

"The bar looks awfully busy, considering it's not even noon yet," she said to Sean.

She and her partner were sitting in an SUV parked at the edge of the bar's lot, observing the establishment. The Rusty Sprocket was a weathered, single-story building that had seen better days, its wooden exterior faded and chipped. A neon sign flickered above the entrance, while a row of grimy windows offered a partial view of the dimly lit interior. Behind the bar stood a forest, the dense tree line stretching out as far as the eye could see.

Still fresh in her mind was Lenny Furtich's warning that Grady Jenkins and his friends would probably be spoiling for a fight. To avoid confrontation, Peyton and Sean had opted for plainclothes instead of their usual NPS uniforms. They wore jeans, t-shirts, and jackets—a stark contrast to the black leather and bandanas adorning the bikers visible through the windows.

"Look at that logo," Sean said, pointing at one of the bikes. On its side was a snarling dog, its eyes glowing red, surrounded by a ring of fire. "These guys must be Hellhounds."

"Can't say I've heard of them," Peyton replied, her voice laced with curiosity.

"They're a rough group, always in trouble with the law—robberies, assaults, and even a couple of murders. They have no respect for authority."

"Great," Peyton muttered, her heart rate quickening. "What are our chances of having a peaceful conversation with Grady, then?"

"Probably not great," Sean admitted, his eyes scanning the motorcycles and the bar's entrance. "We need to be ready for anything, including a fight."

Peyton took a deep breath and mentally prepared herself for the confrontation that might ensue. She knew the importance of finding Grady Jenkins, but the thought of facing off against an entire biker gang made her heart race. Still, she had been trained for high-stress situations during her time at the FBI. If it came down to it, she was ready.

Together, they stepped out of the SUV and approached the bar. The worn wooden door creaked as they pushed it open, revealing the grungy interior of the Rusty Sprocket. The air inside was thick with the scent of stale beer, cigarette smoke, and sweat. It was far from inviting, but they had come this far, and there was no turning back.

The bar itself was a long, battered slab of wood, its surface stained and scarred from years of use. Old neon signs advertising various brands of beer cast a flickering, multicolored glow on the walls, which were covered in tattered posters and graffiti. A jukebox in one corner played classic rock tunes, the music barely audible over the din of voices and laughter.

As they entered, Peyton couldn't help but notice the numerous Hellhound members scattered throughout the room. They were a rough-looking bunch, their bodies adorned with tattoos and piercings, faces weathered by years of hard living. Leather jackets emblazoned with their gang's insignia hung from the backs of chairs or were draped over their broad shoulders.

As soon as Peyton and Sean crossed the threshold, the Hellhounds stopped what they were doing and studied them. The cold way the bikers watched Peyton and Sean made Peyton feel like a piece of meat being sized up by a pack of hungry wolves. She fought to suppress the shiver that ran down her spine and tried to project an air of confidence, even as she felt anything but.

Peyton and Sean approached the bar, its worn wooden surface stained with years of spilled drinks and rough use. The bartender's face was a roadmap of hard experiences. His eyes were sunken, surrounded by wrinkles like spiderwebs, and his stubble-covered jaw was set in a perpetual scowl. His arms, covered in faded tattoos, told a story of their own.

"Two coffees," Peyton said as steadily as she could. "And whatever you have for breakfast."

The bartender just stared at her, his expression unchanging. Their plainclothes might hide the fact that they were rangers, but it didn't hide the fact that they were outsiders here.

"Sorry, sweetheart," a bald biker with a bushy beard and an array of piercings said from a nearby table, "but this is a private establishment. Members only." His lip curled into a sneer, revealing yellowed teeth. "And I can tell you ain't members."

"Look, we don't want any trouble," Sean said, his hand resting on Peyton's shoulder. She could feel his fingers pressing into her skin, a silent reminder that they needed to watch each other's backs.

In a low voice, the bartender leaned in closer, his breath smelling of stale whiskey and cigarettes. "I suggest you two leave," he warned, his eyes darting around the room. "I don't want another fight here—I've had enough of those to last me a lifetime."

"Listen," Sean said, his voice equally hushed, "we just need to talk to a guy named Grady Jenkins. Once we've done that, we'll be out of your hair, promise."

The bartender looked like he was about to say something when his gaze suddenly shifted, focusing on something behind Peyton and Sean. His expression stiffened.

"Is there a problem here?" came a gravelly voice from behind them. Peyton turned around to see the bald biker standing behind them, grinning menacingly. His grin revealed a mouth full of crooked teeth, and his eyes seemed to gleam with malice. The biker's muscles rippled beneath his leather vest, adorned with various patches that hinted at a history of violence.

"Say, what are you two doin' here?" the biker asked mockingly, his voice heavy with suspicion. He crossed his arms over his broad chest and eyed them up and down.

Peyton decided honesty was the best policy in this situation. "We're looking for Grady Jenkins," she said.

"Are you cops?" The biker raised an eyebrow, his grin widening. Several heads turned in their direction, conversations around the room coming to a halt.

"No," Sean replied, shooting a quick glance at Peyton before turning back to the biker. "We're with the National Park Service."

"Rangers, huh?" The biker laughed loudly, the sound carrying throughout the room. "You know, I've never been too fond of rangers. Always stickin' their noses in where they don't belong, tryin' to ruin everyone's fun." He spat on the floor, narrowly missing Sean's boot.

Peyton bristled at the biker's disdain but forced herself to remain calm, not wanting to escalate the situation any further. She knew they were trespassing on dangerous ground, and one wrong move could send everything spiraling out of control. Instead, she scanned the room, trying to discern which of these men might be Grady Jenkins.

Then she spotted a slim, tattooed man with a scruffy beard and closely cropped hair, slipping out the back door. The man wore an air of nonchalance, but his hurried pace betrayed his true intentions.

Peyton discreetly patted Sean's shoulder, her heart racing as she leaned in close to his ear. "We need to leave now," she whispered urgently.

"Wha–" Sean began, confusion clouding his face.

"Just trust me," Peyton insisted, her eyes fixed on the door the tattooed man had vanished through.

Reluctantly, Sean nodded. "Sorry to bother you," he said to the bald biker. "We'll hit the road."

To Peyton's relief, no one tried to stop them. She and Sean stepped out of the Rusty Sprocket and into the morning sunlight, which filtered through the treetops with an almost ethereal quality. The parking lot was a sea of chrome and gleaming metal as the motorcycles lined up in neat rows, their polished surfaces reflecting the light. Ignoring the steady hum of conversation from within the bar, Peyton focused her attention on the building's perimeter.

"Follow me," she said as she hurried around the corner of the weathered structure. The wooden exterior creaked beneath years of exposure to the elements, its paint flaking away in places like the shed skin of some ancient creature.

Sean followed close behind, his brow furrowed in concern. "What's going on?" he asked, keeping his voice low.

"I think I may have found Grady," she replied, her eyes scanning their surroundings for any sign of the tattooed man who had slipped out of the back door moments earlier. She spotted him walking briskly toward the woods, his pace purposeful and determined.

"Come on," she whispered, breaking into a quiet jog as she followed the tattooed man from a safe distance. Sean fell in step beside her, his face set in a grim expression as they plunged into the forest together.

The world seemed to change as they entered the woods, the air growing cooler and damper, the sunlight less brilliant as it filtered through the dense canopy above. Fallen leaves crunched beneath their feet, their damp, earthy scent clinging to the air. Around them, tree trunks loomed like silent sentinels, bearing witness to their pursuit.

"Where did he go?" Sean asked, his breath visible in the crisp air as he scanned the area, searching for any trace of the tattooed man. His sudden disappearance was disconcerting, and Peyton couldn't help but feel a sense of unease creeping over her.

"Shh," she hushed him, tilting her head to listen. The forest seemed unnaturally quiet, as if it were holding its breath in anticipation. Had the tattooed man sprinted as soon as he entered the woods? Or had he hidden himself among the undergrowth, waiting to ambush them?

The sound of a twig snapping underfoot broke through the stillness, making Peyton's heart pound in her chest. She spun around, her instincts on high alert as she found herself face-to-face with the tattooed man she had been quietly trailing. His eyes were dark and menacing, his lean, muscular frame tense with aggression. The jagged lines of a serpent tattoo snaked up his exposed forearm, disappearing beneath the worn leather vest that hugged his broad shoulders.

"Why are you following me?" he demanded, the cold steel of a knife glinting in his hand as he pointed it at her.

"Put down the knife," Sean said, drawing his weapon. But the man paid him no heed, his gaze fixed solely on Peyton, as if he could see straight into her soul.

"Are you Grady Jenkins?" Peyton asked.

The man shook his head, but his silence spoke volumes. It was clear that he knew where Grady was—and that he had no intention of telling them.

"Why are you looking for him?" the man asked.

"Grady's ex-girlfriend was killed recently," Peyton said. "We need to talk to him about it."

"Think he did it?" the man sneered, his grip tightening around the knife handle.

"We don't know what to think," Sean said. "That's why we need to talk to him." He was holding his gun in both hands, aiming at the stranger's chest.

For a moment, the man hesitated, seemingly weighing his options. It was then that a rustle of leaves caught his attention, the sound of two squirrels chasing each other through the undergrowth momentarily distracting him from the tense standoff.

Seizing her opportunity, Peyton lunged forward. With a swift, decisive motion, she grabbed the man's wrist and twisted it sharply, using his own momentum to force him to drop the knife.

The man cried out in pain, wincing as he cradled his wrist.

"Nice move," Sean murmured to Peyton, holstering his gun.

Peyton picked up the fallen knife and slipped it into her pocket. "Thanks." Her gaze bore into the tattooed man, scrutinizing his every move. "How about you tell us what you're doing out here in the woods?" she asked.

The man remained sullen and silent, refusing to meet her eyes. That didn't deter her, however. "Were you going to warn Grady?" she asked, noting the way his jaw clenched at the mention of the name.

Still, the man said nothing, his silence only increasing Peyton's suspicions. She could feel the tension radiating from him, like a tightly coiled spring waiting to snap.

It was then that Sean furrowed his brow and sniffed the air. "Do you smell that?" he asked, his eyes darting around the forest, searching for the source of the scent. "Smoke."

Peyton inhaled deeply, catching the faint whiff of burning wood. "I think you're right," she said, nodding toward a barely visible plume of smoke farther along the trail. "Maybe we should check it out."

"What about our friend?" Sean asked.

She shrugged one shoulder. "We'll find Grady ourselves."

The man hesitated for a moment before slinking away, leaving them alone in the dappled sunlight with only the sounds of birdsong and rustling leaves to accompany them.

As Peyton and Sean continued down the forest trail, the smell of smoke grew stronger, mingling with the earthy scents of damp soil and decaying leaves. Rounding a bend in the trail, Peyton spotted a clearing up ahead. At its center was a huge bonfire, a roaring inferno of orange and red that licked at the sky as if trying to devour it whole.

A number of bikers had gathered around the bonfire, their laughter and chatter carrying through the woods like the rumble of distant thunder. They lounged in lawn chairs, drinking from bottles wrapped in brown paper bags, and seemed to be having a grand old time. Their leather jackets carried various insignias, some bearing the Hellhounds' logo Sean had recognized earlier.

Peyton's gaze flicked between the bikers and the fire, her heart pounding with a mix of adrenaline and trepidation. She couldn't help but notice how dangerously close the flames were to the surrounding trees, the heat causing the dry leaves and branches to shrivel and blacken. Sparks and embers danced like fireflies on the breeze, threatening to ignite the dry undergrowth at any moment.

"Is it legal to build fires here?" she asked Sean.

"Not like this one," he replied, his eyes narrowing as he assessed the situation.

"Somebody should tell them they need to put the fire out."

"Too late," Sean said, pointing. Peyton followed his finger and saw tendrils of fire snaking their way along the ground, consuming the brittle, fallen leaves. If Peyton and Sean didn't do something soon, the whole forest might be on fire in minutes.

CHAPTER NINE

As Peyton and Sean hurried toward the bonfire, a sinking feeling settled in Peyton's gut. The flames were already perilously close to the woods, the nearby leaves beginning to catch fire. She glanced at Sean, who shared her concern. They needed to act fast before the situation escalated out of control.

"Sean, we have to put this fire out!" she called over the crackle of the burning leaves. She racked her brain for a solution as they sprinted closer. It came to her in a flash—they could smother the flames. Surveying the area, she spotted a jacket draped on a nearby chair, hastily abandoned by one of the bikers. Without hesitation, she snatched it up and began using it to beat out the spreading fire.

With each determined swing, the jacket smothered more and more of the hungry flames. Sweat beaded on Peyton's brow as she put her full weight into each blow. Sean acted quickly to assist her. He kicked dirt and stomped on the smaller fires, using his boots to good effect. Together, they were making progress, gradually extinguishing the encroaching fire and containing the danger.

"Keep going, Peyton! We're almost there," Sean shouted, his voice strained with effort.

Just as they seemed to be getting the situation under control, however, a biker in a wife-beater t-shirt approached Peyton angrily. His eyes blazed with fury as he demanded, "What the hell are you doing with my jacket?"

Before Peyton could respond, Sean swiftly intervened, stepping between them. "Back off!" he growled, his face set in a stern expression. "We're putting out a fire that could've burned down this entire place."

The biker crossed his arms, the anger still simmering beneath the surface. "You're gonna pay for my jacket, then. It's ruined now."

Peyton couldn't believe the biker was more concerned about his jacket than the danger they'd just averted. She glanced at Sean, who was trying to reason with him. In the heat of the moment, she found herself admiring his ability to stay calm and collected.

"Look," Sean said, his eyes never leaving the biker's gaze, "we'll deal with the jacket later. Right now, we've got bigger issues to handle. Understood?"

As Sean continued to argue with the biker over the ruined jacket, Peyton couldn't help but feel a growing unease. The inebriated crowd of bikers began to close in around them, their expressions a mix of curiosity and hostility. She knew they had to tread carefully here; any wrong move could lead to an all-out brawl.

"Who are you two?" one of the burlier bikers demanded, his words slurred from alcohol.

"Look," Peyton tried to explain, her voice steady despite the mounting tension, "we're park rangers, and we just put out a fire that could've caused some serious damage. We're not here to cause trouble."

The bikers exchanged skeptical glances, not quite convinced by her explanation. Just then, the tattooed biker Peyton and Sean had questioned earlier returned, a sneer on his face as he addressed the gathering crowd.

"Hey, guys!" he called out. "Those two are cops! They're looking for Grady!"

The atmosphere instantly shifted, the bikers' agitation escalating at the mention of cops. Peyton clenched her fists, frustration bubbling up inside her. They'd come so far, only to be derailed by this misunderstanding.

"We're not cops," she said, raising her voice above the rising clamor. "We're park rangers. There's a difference!"

But it seemed her words fell on deaf ears. The bikers were now practically seething with anger, and it was clear that violence was only a hair's breadth away.

It was then that a large man pushed his way through the throng of bikers, his broad shoulders and imposing stature commanding attention. He had a thick beard and long, unkempt hair, his piercing eyes scanning both Peyton and Sean with undisguised contempt.

"I'm Grady Jenkins," he growled, his voice like gravel. "What do you want with me?"

"Grady," Peyton began, her tone firm despite the trepidation churning in her gut. "Did you know Amanda Torres?"

At the mention of Amanda's name, Grady's eyes narrowed, and he nodded curtly. "Yeah, I knew her. What's it to you?"

"We need to talk to you about her," Peyton replied, trying to maintain an air of authority despite the hostile situation. "It's important."

Grady's expression turned to one of defiance, his stance as solid as a stone wall. "I'm not going anywhere with you two. I don't like rangers. You made a huge mistake coming here."

Peyton could feel the pressure building, the imminent threat of violence growing more palpable by the second. She glanced at Sean, who stood beside her, tense and ready for whatever might come their way. They were outnumbered and surrounded, but they had little choice but to stand their ground.

"We don't want any trouble here," Sean said. "But if you push us, we *will* defend ourselves."

Grady scoffed, his eyes flicking over Peyton and Sean with disdain. "You shouldn't have stuck your noses where they didn't belong."

Peyton's heart raced as she scanned the circle of sneering faces surrounding them. Her hand instinctively sought the cold metal grip of her weapon, ready to draw it if necessary. She hoped it wouldn't come to that, but she knew they had to be prepared for anything.

As if on cue, one of the bikers lunged toward Sean, his grimy hand reaching for the ranger's holstered weapon. Startled, Sean swatted at the man's arm, trying to knock it away, but the biker was persistent. They struggled, each of them vying for control of the gun, their movements frantic and desperate.

"Damn it," Peyton muttered under her breath, drawing her own weapon. She aimed it at the man fighting with Sean, her voice firm as she commanded, "Put your hands up!"

But before the words had fully left her lips, a solid mass slammed into her side, sending her sprawling to the ground. Leaves crunched beneath her as she fell, her gun flying from her grasp and disappearing into a nearby pile of foliage.

"Son of a—" she gasped, pain radiating through her body. Gritting her teeth, she pushed herself up onto her elbows and looked around. Several bikers were advancing toward her, their expressions a mix of anger and anticipation. They were clearly spoiling for a fight.

"Really?" she taunted, her voice laced with disdain as she slowly rose to her feet, her muscles tensing, preparing for the inevitable confrontation. "Three against one? Is that really fair?"

"What," one of them sneered, his voice thick with mockery, "worried you'll break a nail?"

A surge of adrenaline coursed through Peyton's veins as one of the bikers lunged at her. Her training kicked in, and she sidestepped his charge, grabbing his arm and using his own momentum to send him sprawling face-first into the ground. She didn't have time to celebrate her victory, however, as another biker rushed her with a switchblade glinting menacingly in the firelight.

"Come on, little girl," he taunted, sweat glistening on his forehead as he circled her like a predator stalking its prey.

"Let's dance," Peyton replied, her voice cold and steady. She had faced dangerous criminals before; this man didn't scare her. As he lunged at her with the knife, she twisted her body to avoid the blade and delivered a powerful kick to his chest, sending him stumbling backward. But he was relentless, snarling as he came at her again.

In the midst of the harrowing confrontation, Peyton stole a glance at Sean, needing to know that he was holding his own. Despite the blood streaming from his nose, he fought fiercely against the man who had tried to take his weapon, his eyes focused and determined. It was a small comfort in the chaos that surrounded them.

With a renewed sense of determination, Peyton turned her attention back to the switchblade-wielding biker. Blocking out everything else, she relied on her instincts and training to guide her movements, each dodge, parry, and counterattack executed with precision. The man finally faltered, giving Peyton the opening she needed to disarm him, twisting his wrist until the knife clattered to the ground. A swift elbow to his temple knocked him unconscious, and he crumpled like a ragdoll at her feet.

Her heart still pounding, Peyton barely had a moment to catch her breath before she found herself facing Grady Jenkins himself. His eyes burned with rage and eagerness to teach her a lesson, his hulking frame casting an imposing shadow in the flickering light of the fire.

"Should've stayed out of this, girl," he growled, pulling a pair of brass knuckles from his pocket and slipping them onto his meaty fingers with a sinister grin.

"Too late for that now," Peyton retorted, her voice edged with steel as she braced herself for the fight of her life. She knew that Grady wouldn't go down without a brutal struggle—but neither would she.

As Grady charged at her like a raging bull, Peyton's foot shot out in a powerful kick aimed at Grady's midsection, but the blow seemed to have little effect on the burly biker. Clad in thick leather and built like an ox, he merely grunted as he absorbed the impact, his sneer never leaving his face.

"Is that all you've got?" Grady taunted, his brass knuckles glinting menacingly in the flickering light of the fire.

Realizing brute force alone wouldn't be enough to take him down, Peyton backpedaled, her mind racing as she tried to think of a way to turn the tables on her opponent. She'd always prided herself on her resourcefulness and adaptability, but now she felt at a loss. What could she do to turn things around?

As Grady charged toward her once more, a wild swing of his fist sent her sprawling to the ground, pain blossoming in her jaw where his brass knuckles had grazed her. Her breath caught in her throat, and for a moment, the world spun around her. But even as Grady loomed over her, preparing to strike again, Peyton's keen eyes spotted a potential weapon: a chunk of smoldering wood from the still-burning bonfire.

Gritting her teeth against the searing heat, she snatched up the wood and swung it with all her might, smashing it against Grady's head just as he lunged toward her. The impact was accompanied by a sizzle and the acrid smell of charred flesh, and Grady stumbled back, dazed and howling in pain.

Seizing the opportunity, Peyton scrambled to her feet and pulled out her handcuffs, her voice steely as she stood over the disoriented biker. "Grady Jenkins, you're under arrest."

Her heart pounded in her chest as she prepared to snap the cuffs onto Grady's wrists, but a sudden rustling sound behind her made her whirl around just in time to see another biker swinging a bottle at her head. Instinctively, she raised her arms to shield herself, but before the blow could land, Sean was there.

In one smooth motion, he caught the man's wrist, delivered a swift knee to his groin, and shoved him aside, leaving the would-be assailant groaning on the ground.

"Nice timing," Peyton said, impressed by Sean's swift intervention as she turned back to Grady, who still seemed disoriented from the blow to his head. She snapped the cold metal handcuffs around Grady's massive wrists. As she tightened them, he sneered at her, his eyes burning with a dangerous intensity.

"You'll regret this," he growled, his voice low and menacing. "My people will come after you when you least expect it."

CHAPTER TEN

"How's the nose?" Peyton asked Sean as she handed him a pack of ice. She picked up a rag and went back to polishing her gun, which had gotten smeared with mud after flying from her hands during the fight with Grady Jenkins and his pals.

"Been better," he replied, gingerly pressing the ice against his bruised and swollen nose. Though not broken, it was clear he'd taken a solid hit. A split lip added to the damage, giving his face a battered appearance.

"How's your jaw?" he asked.

She shrugged. "Wasn't a solid hit. I'll be fine." Even as she spoke the words, she took a moment to assess her own injuries, realizing that she'd fared better than Sean. Her knuckles were scraped and bruised, her jaw burned where the brass knuckles had grazed her, and a dull ache throbbed in her ribs where Grady had struck her. But overall, she knew she'd been lucky.

They were in a ranger station only a few miles from the Rusty Sprocket. Grady Jenkins, Amanda Torres's abusive ex-boyfriend and biker gang member, was currently waiting in another room, handcuffed and no doubt fuming. Peyton glanced around their temporary base of operations, taking in the sturdy wooden walls adorned with maps of the park and various wildlife posters. A few worn desks and filing cabinets were scattered about, giving the space a functional yet cluttered atmosphere.

"Thanks again for stepping in back there," she said to Sean. "That biker could've done some serious damage with that bottle if you hadn't acted so quickly."

Sean shrugged it off, the gesture accompanied by a wry smile. "That's what partners do," he said. He cleared his throat. "Ready to talk to our friend?"

"Let's do it," Peyton agreed, steeling herself for the confrontation ahead.

As they entered the small, windowless room, they found Grady sitting at a metal table, his hands cuffed in front of him. His head hung low, making it difficult to discern any emotions on his face. A dim overhead light cast harsh shadows across the room, amplifying the somber atmosphere.

Grady's imposing figure was even more intimidating up close, his muscular arms and broad chest a testament to his brute strength. A few fresh cuts and bruises adorned his face, consequences of the scuffle earlier. But it was his eyes that held Peyton's attention: dark, cold, and defiant.

"Can we get you anything, Mr. Jenkins?" Peyton asked, trying to maintain an air of professionalism. She knew that getting through to him wouldn't be easy, but she had to try.

"You can get the hell out of my face," he said.

"Is that any way to talk to a lady?" Sean chimed in, raising an eyebrow at Grady's crude behavior.

"Ha!" Grady scoffed, glaring at Peyton. "She ain't no lady. Ladies don't fight dirty."

"Sometimes, fighting dirty is the only option," Peyton said. She sat down across from Grady, folding her hands on the table. "Now tell me. When did you last see Amanda Torres?"

"Can't remember," he muttered, refusing to meet her gaze. It was clear he wasn't making any effort to recall the memory.

"You really think lying to us is a good idea?" Sean asked. "If you don't start talking, you could be facing murder charges."

"Murder?" Grady's eyes widened, his tough demeanor momentarily crumbling as shock registered on his face. "You're telling me Amanda's dead?"

"Unfortunately, yes," Peyton said, watching as Grady processed the information. "Why did you think we were asking about her?"

"Figured that new boyfriend of hers, Lenny, sent you to cause trouble for me," he replied, still visibly shaken by the news. "But...murder? I can't believe she's gone."

Peyton studied Grady's face carefully, trying to discern if his shock was genuine or if it was all an act. During her career in law enforcement, she'd encountered her fair share of criminals who could play the part of the grieving friend or lover with chilling accuracy.

Is that what Grady was doing now?

"What happened to her?" Grady asked in a low voice.

It was Sean who answered. "She drowned in the Ember River."

Upon hearing this, Grady's face crumpled, and tears began streaming down his cheeks. His broad shoulders shook as he sobbed uncontrollably, burying his face in his hands.

Peyton watched him closely, shocked by the sudden transformation. Something about Grady's reaction felt raw and real.

"Grady," Sean spoke up after allowing him a moment to compose himself, "where were you yesterday morning?"

"Wh-what?" Grady stammered through his tears. "I was..." Grady's voice cracked. "I was at my sister's house. She needed help fixing her car." He sniffled, wiping tears from his eyes with the back of his hand. "You can ask her if you don't believe me."

"We'll do that," Sean said. "You've gotta admit, though, this is looking pretty bad for you. We have police reports indicating you slapped Amanda around on more than one occasion. And now she's dead, drowned in a river." Sean leaned in closer to Grady, his voice low and menacing. "You better start telling us the truth, Grady. It's your only chance to avoid a lifetime behind bars."

Grady looked up at Sean, his eyes bloodshot and pleading. "I didn't do it," he said, his voice shaking with emotion. "I loved Amanda. Even after we broke up, I still cared about her. I didn't want her to end up with that loser Lenny."

"Lenny didn't kill her," Sean said, his patience wearing thin. "You, on the other hand..." He held out his hands, as if to say there was on telling one way or the other.

Peyton watched as Grady's face contorted with anger and frustration. She could tell he was on the brink of losing control.

"You know what?" Grady spat, slamming his fists onto the table. "I'm done with this! I didn't kill Amanda, and I'm not gonna sit here and let you accuse me of it!" He pushed his chair back, standing up with a force that made the metal legs screech across the floor.

Peyton stood up as well, her hand reaching for her gun instinctively. "Grady, calm down," she said, trying to defuse the situation. "We just want to find out what happened to her."

"I didn't kill her!" he roared, shoving the table aside. "I loved her, damn it! Why would I kill her?"

"That's what we're trying to figure out," Peyton said calmly. "We need to know everything you know about Amanda's disappearance and death. Every detail is important."

Grady took a deep breath, his fists still clenched. "I don't know anything," he said, his voice quieter now. "I haven't seen her in weeks. She...she didn't want to see me. I tried calling her, texting her, but she didn't respond. I figured she was just trying to move on, trying to forget about me and what I did to her." He hung his head, his voice barely a whisper. "I never meant to hurt her, you know. I was just...angry. Things got out of control."

"What things?" Peyton asked, her voice gentle now. "What did you do to Amanda?"

Grady looked up at her, his eyes haunted. "We got into a fight," he said slowly. "About Lenny. Amanda was seeing him, and I didn't like it. I thought he was bad news, that he was just using her for her money. We argued, and...I lost my temper." He paused, swallowing hard. "I hit her. I didn't mean to, but I did. And then she left, and I never saw her again."

Peyton could see the guilt and pain etched on Grady's face. It was clear he regretted what he had done to Amanda, and she wondered if he was telling the truth about not killing her. But there was still so much they didn't know, so much that didn't add up.

If Grady and Amanda had fought about Lenny, then why had Amanda and Lenny continued to keep their relationship a secret? Maybe, she supposed, Amanda had wanted Grady to believe she'd stopped seeing Lenny, just so that he wouldn't bother them.

"Can you think of anyone who might have wanted to harm Amanda?" Peyton asked, her voice tinged with disappointment. She had hoped that Grady would be the key to solving this case, but his alibi and apparent devastation at Amanda's death suggested otherwise.

Grady shook his head, wiping away fresh tears from his reddened eyes. "No," he said. "I can't think of anyone."

Peyton observed him for a moment, sensing his turmoil. "Alright," she said finally. "We'll give you some space."

As Peyton and Sean got up to leave the room, Grady called out to them. "How did Amanda drown?"

Sean glanced back at him, his face somber. "We don't know yet."

"Odd," Grady muttered.

"Why's that?" Peyton asked.

Grady's brow furrowed. "I just remember hearing about another woman who almost drowned three months ago in the Ember River. Julia Raimi, I think it was."

"Almost drowned?" Sean asked. "How'd that happen?"

Grady leaned back, looking thoughtful. "From what I heard, it wasn't an accident. Someone didn't want her to make it out of that river alive."

CHAPTER ELEVEN

Arnold approached the golf cart barn with calculated steps, his eyes darting back and forth, surveying the area for any signs of unexpected company. The barn was quiet, devoid of the usual bustle and chatter of employees or golfers preparing for a round. It was the perfect opportunity.

Stepping inside the wooden structure, Arnold could smell gasoline mingling with the faint scent of leather from the seats. Rows of sleek golf carts lined the interior, their metal frames gleaming under the sharp fluorescent lighting. He crouched low, creeping along the line of carts, each one tempting him like a shiny new toy. His heart hammered as he considered the possibilities laid out before him.

As Arnold's fingers grazed the cold metal frame of one particular cart, he knew this was the one. Its dark green color would allow it to blend effortlessly with the surrounding foliage in the park. This would give him the advantage he needed while stalking his prey. It was also a plus that the tires were larger than those on other carts, which made the cart better suited to handle the uneven terrain that lay ahead.

Arnold pulled out a set of keys he had copied earlier. It had been surprisingly easy; all it had taken was a momentary distraction of the maintenance worker who held the original set. In that brief window, he had managed to take an imprint of the keys using a small piece of clay he carried with him. Later, at a locksmith shop, he acquired his own set without raising any suspicion.

With the keys in hand, Arnold looked around one last time, ensuring he was still alone. He felt a surge of excitement course through his veins as he anticipated the thrill of the hunt. A smile crossed his lips as he thought about the unsuspecting prey that awaited him in the campground. Everything was falling into place, and soon he would be free to indulge his darkest desires.

Just as Arnold was about to twist the key, however, the sound of the barn door creaking open pierced the silence. He froze, his breath caught in his throat, as two employees entered. They were a mismatched pair – one tall and lanky, the other short and stocky – both dressed in green maintenance uniforms.

"Man, you should've seen it," the taller employee said, laughing. "Old Man Roberts tried to take a shortcut across the water hazard on the eighth hole, but his golf cart got stuck right in the middle of the pond!"

The shorter employee snorted, trying to stifle his laughter. "Did he really think he could make it across without sinking?"

"Guess so," the taller one replied, shaking his head. "It took us an hour to fish him and the cart out of there. He was soaked to the bone, and boy, was he mad!"

As they continued chatting, oblivious to Arnold's presence, he held his breath, praying they wouldn't notice him. His heart felt like it would burst from his chest as he watched them walk farther into the barn, their laughter bouncing off the walls.

Finally, the pair climbed into a nearby golf cart, still chuckling at the absurdity of Old Man Roberts' misadventure. With a hum, the cart came to life, and they drove out of the building. As the sound of the engine faded into the distance, Arnold released a long, shaky breath, his body trembling with relief.

With the coast now clear, Arnold wasted no time in starting his own golf cart. The low rumble of the engine under his fingertips served as a reminder of the power he held. Grinning, he steered the cart out of the barn and onto the dirt path that led through the woods.

The afternoon winter sun cast long shadows across the trail, bathing everything in a golden glow. The trees loomed above him, their branches swaying gently in the breeze like ancient sentinels guarding the secrets of the forest. A sense of excitement and eagerness filled Arnold's chest as he navigated the winding path.

Soon, Arnold emerged from the cover of the trees and entered a bustling campground. Families and friends gathered around crackling campfires, the aroma of grilled food filling the air. Children scampered about chasing after one another, their laughter rising above the hum of conversation. The Great Smoky Mountains National Park was a popular destination, especially with the unseasonably warm weather that had settled in for early winter.

Arnold's eyes roamed over the scene. He waved and smiled at a group of campers who greeted him as he passed by, playing the part of a friendly visitor. But beneath the facade, his mind worked furiously, analyzing each person he encountered, searching for the ideal target.

Tents and RVs were scattered haphazardly across the grounds, their inhabitants enjoying the brief respite from the colder months. A group of college students tossed a Frisbee back and forth, their laughter rolling through the clearing. In another corner, a father and son struggled to set up their tent, their frustration evident in their grunts and groans.

Too many witnesses, Arnold thought as he surveyed the area. *I need someone more isolated.*

He continued navigating the golf cart through the maze of tents and vehicles until he spotted a couple in their twenties, talking as they lounged in camp chairs. *Talking*, though, was not really the right word for it—even at a glance, Arnold could tell that the man was doing all the talking and the woman was doing all the listening. The man's chest was puffed out, his arms spread out to either side as if to take up as much space as possible, a beer in either cupholder.

In contrast, the woman sat slump-shouldered, cradling a bottle of water and staring vacantly at the ground. Arnold slowed, trying to hear the man without being too conspicuous.

"I'm just saying," the man said, his tone condescending. "If you would just put in a little more effort, maybe we could have a real vacation. I mean, look around you, all these people are having a great time and you're just sitting there like a lump."

The woman sighed, looking up at him with a defeated expression. "I'm sorry, Caden. I'll try to have more fun."

Pathetic, Arnold thought, shaking his head.

"I'm just looking out for your best interests," the man continued. "You get so stuck in your feelings that you lose the forest for the trees. Come on, have a beer. It'll help you lighten up."

The woman went rigid. "You know I don't drink, not since what happened with my dad."

"Come on, that was ages ago. You think one beer is gonna turn you into your old man? Don't be so stupid, Chloe."

Chloe rose abruptly, her cheeks flaming red. "I need to take a walk, get some air."

Caden waved at her, disgusted. "Yeah, yeah. Just be back by dinner. I invited some of the guys over, and you know you make the best campfire nachos."

Chloe said nothing. She just started walking off, the disappointment in her gait obvious. Caden shot her a nasty glare before returning to his beer, his face brightening as he struck up a conversation with a man walking past him.

Arnold watched Chloe disappear into the trees, his expression changing to one of barely contained glee. He'd found his target.

I could use a little fresh air, too, Arnold thought, pulling forward and following Chloe from a distance, careful not to arouse suspicion as the sounds of laughter and music died behind him.

Chloe took a winding dirt path leading deeper into the woods, her pace steady but unhurried. Arnold remained vigilant, staying far enough back that she wouldn't feel threatened but close enough to keep her in sight. Every now and then, she glanced over her shoulder, her expression growing increasingly uneasy. He could sense her fear, and it only fueled his desire.

Good, he thought, *she knows I'm here. Let her be afraid.*

The trail narrowed, the trees closing in around them as they ventured further into the forest. Arnold decided it was time to make his move. He accelerated the golf cart, catching up to Chloe until they were side by side.

Now that he was closer, he noticed the delicate features of her face—high cheekbones, large green eyes framed by thick lashes, and full, pink lips. Her chestnut hair was pulled back into a messy ponytail, stray wisps clinging to her sweat-dampened forehead. She was undeniably beautiful, but that only served to fuel his animosity toward her.

"Hey, there," Arnold called out, feigning friendliness. "Need a lift?"

Chloe looked at him cautiously, her eyes narrowing as she took in his appearance. "No, thank you," she replied, her voice wavering slightly. "I'm fine walking."

"Are you sure?" Arnold pressed, injecting concern into his tone. "You look like you could use a break. I don't mind giving you a ride."

For a moment, she hesitated, clearly weighing her options. But ultimately, the mistrust in her eyes won out. "Really, I'm okay," she insisted, her pace quickening as she broke into a light jog.

"Suit yourself," he muttered under his breath. He accelerated the golf cart, his eyes locked on Chloe as she jogged ahead of him. A bead of sweat trickled down his temple, the cool air rushing past him. This was the perspiration of excitement, a visceral reaction to the hunt.

"Hey!" he called out, raising his voice to be heard over the hum of the electric motor. "You really should get rid of that deadbeat boyfriend of yours! He's no good for you."

She glanced back at the man, her green eyes wide with panic. "Just leave me alone," she panted, her breath ragged as she pushed herself to run faster.

"Sorry, sweetheart," Arnold replied, grinning wickedly as his heart pounded in his chest. "I can't do that."

"Wh-why not?" she stammered.

"I would tell you," he said, "but that would take all the fun out of it, now wouldn't it?"

As the words left his lips, he saw her terror increase tenfold. Her once rosy cheeks were now pallid, and sweat dripped down her neck, soaking the collar of her shirt. Arnold reveled in her distress—it was like a drug, making him feel more alive than ever before.

Then, without warning, Chloe veered off the trail, darting into the dense underbrush that lined the path. Arnold slammed on the brakes and leaped from the golf cart, his pulse racing as he chased after her.

The woods swallowed them up, the twisted branches and thorny vines clawing at Arnold's skin as he fought through the brush. The damp earth squelched beneath his boots, and the pungent scent of decaying leaves filled his nostrils. He could hear her frantic gasps for air, the snap of twigs beneath her feet, and with each sound, his excitement surged.

"Running won't save you!" he shouted, his voice breaking through the trees. The thrill of the chase consumed him, driving him deeper into the forest. He could feel the distance between them shrinking, and as he gained on her, an image formed in his mind—the look of pure terror on her face when he finally caught her.

"Please," she sobbed, stumbling over a tangled root as she glanced back at him. "Please, don't hurt me!"

"Too late for that," Arnold growled, the fire in his belly raging as he closed in on her, his resolve unshakable. He would make her understand why she couldn't escape him, why he had chosen her.

He lunged forward, his fingers brushing against Chloe's sweat-soaked shirt. They tumbled to the ground together, a mass of limbs and desperate gasps for breath. Her eyes were wide with terror, her chest heaving with the exertion of their chase.

"Get off me!" she screamed, her fingers clawing at Arnold's grip on her arm. He could feel the primal fear pulsing through her veins, feeding his own desires. He tightened his hold, relishing in the power he held over her.

"Stop struggling," he hissed, the words dripping with venom. "You can't escape me."

"What do you want from me?" she choked out between sobs, her entire body trembling beneath him. Arnold's eyes roamed over her face, taking in every detail—the way her mascara had smeared beneath her tear-filled eyes, the flush of her cheeks, the way her lips quivered with each pained cry.

Ignoring her question, Arnold maneuvered himself into position, slipping one arm around her neck and tightening it into a vice-like headlock. Chloe's fingers grasped wildly at his arm, her nails digging into his flesh as she struggled for air. But Arnold only tightened his grip.

"Please," she wheezed, her voice barely a whisper. "Please, let me go."

"Can't you see?" Arnold whispered into her ear. "This is for your own good. Soon, it'll all make sense—I promise."

CHAPTER TWELVE

"There's one thing I can't figure," Peyton said as she and Sean walked toward the apartment complex, her brow furrowed in deep thought. "If the killer really did attack Julia, why not come back for her? Why leave unfinished business?"

The apartment complex loomed before them, a series of gray, dilapidated buildings that seemed to sag under the weight of their own decay. The area was clearly impoverished, with peeling paint and cracked windows marring the façade of each structure. The air was thick with the smell of grease and cigarette smoke, the cacophony of loud music and children's laughter echoing through the narrow alleys that twisted their way between buildings.

As they navigated the maze-like pathways, they passed clusters of residents huddled together on stoops and balconies, their eyes following the newcomers with guarded curiosity. A mangy dog barked at them from behind a chain-link fence, its ribs visible beneath its matted fur. An unsettling feeling of desperation hung in the air, making it clear that this is not a place where hope thrived.

"Maybe the killer thought he'd succeeded," Sean said, his voice steady despite the unsettling surroundings. "He could have assumed she drowned and didn't bother to check up on her."

"Or maybe he's just biding his time, waiting for the right moment to strike again," Peyton countered, her gaze flicking between the faces of those they passed.

"Either way," Sean continued, "as far as we know, Julia's near-drowning was simply an accident, and the rest is just rumor. We need to find out what really happened before we start jumping to conclusions."

They finally reached Julia Raimi's apartment door. It stood out as a dull and worn wooden slab, paint peeling from its surface to reveal the years of neglect it had endured. The once vibrant blue color was now a muted grayish hue. Beside the door, a small window covered with a dirty, tattered curtain allowed for a glimpse into the dark world inside. The hallway leading up to the apartment reeked of stale cigarettes and dampness, amplifying the oppressive atmosphere that seemed to envelop them.

"Here goes nothing," Peyton muttered before knocking on the door, her knuckles rapping against the rough wood. There was no answer, only the muffled sound of their own breathing in the stifling air.

Peyton scanned the area and noticed a neighbor sitting nearby. She was an older woman, her face etched with lines of hardship and time, dressed in a faded floral housecoat. A lit cigarette dangled precariously from her thin lips as she watched them intently from the shadows.

"Excuse me," Peyton said, trying to appear friendly despite her growing unease. "Do you know if Julia is home?"

The woman took her time, inhaling deeply before exhaling a plume of smoke in their direction. Her eyes narrowed as she studied them. "You cops?" she asked, her voice raspy from years of smoking.

Peyton looked down at their plainclothes, realizing they hadn't changed back into uniform since entering the Rusty Sprocket to find Grady Jenkins. "No, we're with the National Park Service," she explained, hoping that would be enough to gain the woman's trust.

"National Park Service, huh?" The woman skeptically eyed them, taking another drag from her cigarette. "What do you want with Julia?"

Sean stepped forward, projecting a calm confidence. "We just need to ask her a few questions about an incident that happened a while back. It's important."

"Good luck with that," the woman snorted, flicking ash onto the floor. "Julia doesn't like visitors. She's pretty much a recluse. Even if she is home, she probably won't let you in."

"Any idea why she keeps to herself like that?" Peyton asked.

The woman shrugged, taking a final drag from her cigarette before stubbing it out on the wall. "Who knows? People around here have their reasons for hiding." She hesitated for a moment, as if weighing whether to share more. "Some say it's got something to do with that drowning incident, but I don't know for sure."

Peyton exchanged a glance with Sean, who raised his eyebrows.

Determined to get answers, Peyton knocked on the door again, louder this time. "Julia, I know you're in there," she called out, hoping she was right. "We just want to talk."

Sean shifted his weight from one foot to the other, looking uneasy. "Maybe she's not home, Peyton," he suggested quietly, glancing around the hallway. Its peeling paint and flickering lights created an unsettling atmosphere that seemed to seep into their bones.

"Give her a moment," Peyton said, her eyes fixated on the door. She'd come too far to give up now. And then, as if to reward her patience, a slight rustle caught her attention. The curtain beside the door twitched ever so slightly, revealing a pair of wide, fearful eyes that quickly disappeared back into the shadows.

"Who are you?" a shaky voice demanded from the other side of the door. "What do you want?"

"We're with the National Park Service," Peyton said, trying to keep her tone soothing. "We just want to ask you a few questions about the incident at the Ember River three months ago. We're not here to cause you any trouble."

"I already talked to the police," Julia replied. "I don't have anything else to say."

"Please," Sean interjected, his voice low and earnest. "We're not trying to upset you. We just need to go over a few more details. There may be a connection between your experience and some recent events in the park. If you could help us, it would mean a lot."

Silence hung heavy in the air for several long moments before the sound of locks disengaging filled the hallway. The door creaked open a fraction, and a woman peered out at them warily. Her dark hair was pulled back into a messy bun, and her eyes were a striking shade of green that seemed to glow in the dim light. Her face was pale and drawn, revealing the weight of the trauma she had endured.

"Are you Julia Raimi?" Peyton asked, taking in the woman's nervous demeanor.

The woman hesitated for a moment before nodding. "What recent events are you talking about?"

Peyton decided to be open. "Two other women have drowned recently, and we're not convinced they were accidents. In fact, we're pretty sure there was foul play."

Julia stared blankly at them for a few seconds. Then, without a word, she retreated into the house, leaving the door open behind her. Sensing this was an invitation, Peyton pushed the door and entered the apartment.

The interior of Julia's apartment was a stark contrast to the chaos outside. The cramped space seemed to be drowning in shadows, with only a single window providing a dim source of light. The furniture was sparse and mismatched, as though it had all been gathered from various second-hand stores. Stacks of newspapers, books, and unopened mail littered nearly every surface, creating a sense of claustrophobia.

"Sorry about the mess," Julia muttered, picking up an armful of clothes from a chair and dumping them in a corner. "I haven't had much motivation to clean lately. Please, have a seat."

Peyton and Sean carefully maneuvered through the clutter to sit on the aged sofa, its cushions flattened by years of use. Peyton tried to ignore the musty smell that lingered in the room.

Julia sat down opposite them in a chair with a lumpy cushion. "Why do you want to know?" she asked with a sigh.

"Tell us what happened three months ago at Great Smoky Mountains National Park," Peyton said. "As best you can remember."

Julia hesitated, her hands nervously twisting in her lap. It was clear that she was terrified, but there was also a spark of determination hidden deep within her eyes. After several long moments, she finally spoke.

"I went there to try and clear my head," she began, her voice wavering but growing stronger with each word. "I had been in a terrible relationship with my boyfriend at the time. He…he took advantage of me, emotionally and financially. I couldn't seem to find the strength to leave him, no matter how much he hurt me."

As Julia spoke, Peyton felt an overwhelming surge of compassion for this broken woman before her. She could see the pain that still haunted her and the bravery it took to share her story.

"What happened that day?" Sean asked gently.

Shadows stretched long across the apartment floor as the afternoon sun began to dip lower in the sky, casting a golden glow through the room's only window. The air inside was heavy and warm, an unusual contrast to the crisp chill of early winter just beyond the door. Peyton watched Julia closely as she gathered herself, preparing to share the events that led to her near-drowning.

"That day," she said, "I was alone in the park because I wanted to get away from everything—my boyfriend, my life, all of it. I just needed some time to think about what I really wanted." Her voice trembled slightly, but she continued, determination in her eyes. "I was hiking one of the trails when this man came up to me. He introduced himself as Guy."

"Did he give you a last name?" Sean asked.

"No." She shook her head. "Just Guy. And to be honest, I can't remember many details about him. He seemed pretty average-looking, I guess."

"Anything at all could be helpful," Peyton said, jotting down the name in her notebook.

Julia closed her eyes, trying to recall more information. "He had short brown hair, maybe? Muscular, like he worked out. And he had a tattoo on his arm, I think."

"A tattoo?" Sean asked.

"I can't picture it, but I thought maybe he had one," Julia said miserably. She sighed, frustrated with her own lack of memory. "I'm sorry, that's all I can remember."

"That's alright," Peyton reassured her. "Please continue with your story."

"Okay, so Guy and I ended up hiking together for a little while. He was friendly, maybe a bit too interested in my life, but I didn't really mind at first. I even confided in him about my relationship troubles—how my boyfriend treated me poorly and how trapped I felt. That's when things started to change."

"Change how?" Sean asked, his brow furrowed.

"Guy became really insistent that I promise not to go back to my boyfriend. It was like he suddenly turned into this controlling person. He got pushy, and I just…I didn't want to be around him anymore. That was the whole reason I was out there, to escape that kind of thing, know what I mean?"

"What happened next?" Peyton asked.

Julia's eyes filled with tears as she recalled the terrifying events that followed. "I tried to leave, but that's when he grabbed me. He started choking me and told me he'd kill me if I didn't do exactly what he said."

Peyton felt her heart race in response to Julia's words, anger toward this mysterious Guy bubbling beneath her skin. The air in the apartment seemed to grow heavier as they listened to Julia recount her ordeal, each word painting a vivid picture of the fear she must have experienced.

"Julia," Sean said, "I know this is hard for you, but we need to hear the rest. What happened after he threatened you?"

Tears streamed down Julia's face as she struggled to catch her breath, the weight of her traumatic memories crushing her. Her voice trembled as she said, "I-I can't... It's just too much."

"Hey, it's okay," Peyton reassured her gently, getting up from her seat and grabbing a box of tissues from a nearby shelf. She handed them to Julia, who took them with shaking hands. "Take your time. We're here to help, not to rush you."

Julia wiped away her tears, nodding gratefully. "Thank you." Taking a few deep breaths, she seemed to find the strength to continue.

"Guy...he led me through the woods," Julia began again, her voice steadier this time. "He took me to a cliff overlooking the Ember River. I remember the sound of the water rushing below... It was so loud and powerful."

Peyton pictured the scene in her mind—the dense forest, the steep cliff, the relentless river far below. She could almost feel the fear that must have gripped Julia as she stood there, completely at Guy's mercy.

"Did you try to get away?" Sean asked.

"I did," she admitted, fresh tears welling up in her eyes. "I begged him to let me go, promised I'd never go back to my boyfriend, but he kept saying it was too late."

"And then?" Peyton asked, already knowing the answer but needing to hear it from Julia herself.

"He pushed me, and I fell. I thought I was going to die." She swallowed hard, then continued, her face pale as she relived the terrifying experience. "Everything went black when I hit the water. I must have hit a stone or something because next thing I knew, I was lying on the bank of the river, downstream from where I'd been pushed in."

"Who found you?" Peyton asked.

"It was a group of kayakers," Julia explained, her words spilling out faster now. "They saw me lying there, bruised and bleeding, and they pulled me out of the water." She hesitated for a moment before carefully pulling back her hair to reveal a jagged scar on her scalp. Both Peyton and Sean leaned in for a closer look, their expressions solemn.

"Thank you for sharing your story with us, Julia," Peyton said softly, placing a comforting hand on her arm. As she absorbed Julia's harrowing story, her gut twisted with empathy for the traumatized woman. She couldn't help but wonder if Guy was the same person who had attacked Amanda Torres and Kimberly Saunders. It was a possibility they couldn't ignore, but they needed more detail to be certain.

"Julia," Peyton began, "I know this is difficult, but I want to try something that might help you remember more details about Guy. It's a small memory trick that could give us some valuable information."

"Okay," Julia replied hesitantly, her eyes wary but determined.

"Close your eyes and take a deep breath," Peyton said, her voice soft and reassuring. "Now, I want you to picture yourself back at the park on that day. Focus on the smallest details: the sounds of the birds, the scent of the trees, the feel of the ground beneath your feet. Let those sensory details transport you back to that moment."

Julia followed Peyton's instructions, her breathing deepening as she immersed herself in the memory. Peyton watched her closely, hoping the technique would yield something useful.

"Now, think about Guy," Peyton continued. "What does he look like? What is he wearing? Try to recall any distinguishing features—anything that will help us identify him."

A furrow appeared between Julia's brows, indicating her concentration. Her eyes moved beneath her closed lids as though scanning the scene in her mind.

"His shoes," Julia suddenly whispered, her eyes snapping open. "They were strange...no laces, like moccasins, but they seemed sturdy enough for hiking."

"Good," Peyton said, her heart rate picking up as she jotted down the detail in her notebook. "That's something we can work with. Is there anything else you can remember?"

Julia shook her head, looking apologetic. "I'm sorry, that's all I can recall."

"Hey, don't worry about it," Peyton reassured her. "You've given us more than enough to work with for now. Thank you, Julia."

"One more question," Sean said. "Why did you keep quiet about this? Why didn't you tell the police?"

Julia glanced away as if ashamed. "I guess I worried that if I talked about it, he'd come after me again. But now that it sounds like he's attacked others…" She shuddered. "I just can't let it keep happening."

Peyton nodded. "We appreciate your help. We won't take up any more of your time."

As Peyton and Sean prepared to leave, Julia studied them, her hands wrestling in her lap. "There was one more thing," she said, her eyes glazed with remembered fear.

Peyton and Sean looked back.

"On the cliff edge," Julia said, "before Guy pushed me...he told me something else. I asked him why he was doing this, and he told me I'd brought it on myself. How could he say something like that?"

CHAPTER THIRTEEN

"You know," Sean said, his voice tinged with doubt, "it might not be safe to assume this 'Guy' fellow is still wearing the same shoes after three months."

Peyton studied the computer screen intensely, her eyes tracing the security camera footage of the Great Smoky Mountains National Park parking lot. The afternoon sun cast elongated shadows over the vehicles and the people walking by, their breaths visible in the chilly air. Her gaze lingered on their footwear, searching for any sign of moccasins amidst the sea of hiking boots and sneakers.

"Even if Guy isn't wearing the same shoes he was wearing when he attacked Julia Raimi," Peyton said, "his sense of style probably hasn't changed. Besides, this is our best lead."

They were seated in a small, cluttered office assigned to them at the park's ranger station. File cabinets lined the walls, and stacks of papers covered most surfaces. A single window allowed a glimpse of the vast expanse of trees outside, their branches bearing the first touch of winter frost. The hum of fluorescent lights above filled the silence when they weren't discussing the case.

They had obtained the security footage from the park's administration with permission from the chief ranger, who was eager to help solve the mysterious attacks that had shaken the community. Peyton and Sean had already looked at footage from several other parking lots within the park, noting the few men who wore moccasins but ultimately ruling them out due to their body types not matching Guy's supposed muscular build. Hours of staring at the screen had left Peyton's eyes tired and her patience wearing thin, but she refused to give up.

"Maybe we should consider another lead," Sean suggested, his voice weary but persistent. "I heard a few of the rangers talking about a suspicious-looking man hanging around the Ember River area on several occasions."

"He was described as blond," Peyton said. "Julia's attacker had brown hair."

"So he dyed it," Sean said with a shrug. "It's worth looking into, isn't it?"

Peyton glanced at him, her eyes narrowing in thought. While she appreciated Sean's input, she couldn't ignore the nagging feeling that focusing on the moccasins was crucial. She had learned to trust her instincts over the years, and they had rarely led her astray.

"Let's keep searching for a little while longer," she insisted, her determination unwavering. "I have a gut feeling that we're close to finding something here."

"I really think we should change course."

They stared at one another, neither backing down. Peyton half-expected Sean to leave, saying they could meet back up later. To her surprise, though, he threw up his hands in surrender.

"Alright," he said. "I'll trust you. But I really hope this pans out. Feels like we're looking for the proverbial needle in the proverbial haystack."

Just then, as if fate itself had intervened, Peyton spotted a man who caught her attention. He was walking across the parking lot, his muscular build evident even through the grainy footage. What truly piqued her interest, however, was his footwear: a pair of unmistakable moccasins.

"Wait, look!" she exclaimed, pointing at the screen. She watched intently as the man approached a vehicle, intrigued by the possibility that this could be their suspect. It was a dark green pickup truck, older and well-worn but still sturdy-looking. Its rugged appearance hinted at a life spent traversing rough terrain, not unlike the vast wilderness of the national park.

Peyton scrambled for a pen and notepad. As she jotted down the plate number, she couldn't help but feel a sense of triumph.

"Sometimes, patience pays off," she said, a determined glint in her eyes. "Now let's find out who this man is."

Opening her laptop, Peyton typed the license plate number into the police database search bar, her fingers moving deftly across the keyboard.

"Got another one," Sean said, breaking Peyton's focus as he pointed to a man on the security footage, also wearing footwear that resembled a pair of moccasins. "I'll take a closer look at this guy."

"Good idea," Peyton replied, her gaze returning to her laptop as the search results finally appeared. Scanning the screen, she found the owner of the truck—a man named Samuel Prescott. She clicked on his name, hoping to find any relevant information about him.

As Peyton delved deeper into Samuel's background, her curiosity grew. His social media profile revealed an array of outdoor activities that he enjoyed—hiking, fishing, and camping. It seemed he frequented the national park quite often, which only made her more intrigued. A picture of Samuel showed a muscular build and brown hair, just like Julia Raimi's description of Guy. Her heart raced as she considered the possibility that they had found their man.

"Check this out," she said, her voice wavering with excitement. But Sean didn't respond, too absorbed in his own investigation.

"Sean?" Peyton asked, louder this time. He looked up from his laptop, an eyebrow raised in question.

"Sorry, I was just...what did you find?" he asked, pulling his chair closer to where she sat.

"Samuel Norton, the owner of the truck. His outdoor interests, his build—they all match up with Julia's description," she explained, pointing to the information on her screen. "I think we might have found Guy."

"Let's not jump to conclusions yet," Sean said, but Peyton could see a flicker of hope in his eyes as well. They both knew that this lead was too promising to ignore.

"Right," Peyton agreed, forcing herself to stay focused. "We need to gather more information before we can be sure."

"Keep digging into Samuel's background while I look into this other guy," Sean suggested, sliding back to his own laptop. "We'll compare notes after and see what we've got."

"Deal," Peyton said, her determination only growing stronger. She would not rest until they had uncovered the truth—no matter where it led them.

Peyton's fingers danced across her keyboard as she delved deeper into the life of Samuel Prescott. She found his social media page and scrolled through his posts, pausing to examine pictures of him hiking with friends, attending concerts, and even participating in a local marathon. He seemed to be an outdoors enthusiast, which fit the profile they were after.

"Come on, give me something," she muttered under her breath, frustration mounting as she clicked through more photos and posts. She could feel the seconds ticking by; each moment spent researching felt like an eternity when justice hung in the balance.

Then it happened—a post that made her stomach drop. That morning, around the time Amanda Torres was killed, Samuel Prescott had shared a photo of himself at a charity event, surrounded by dozens of people. The timestamp on the photo matched up perfectly with the time of the murder. It was clear: Samuel couldn't have been responsible for Amanda's death.

"Damn it," Peyton cursed under her breath, her shoulders slumping in defeat. All the hours of work, the meticulous scrutiny of security footage, and the race against time—all for nothing. They had hit yet another dead end.

"Maybe this was a waste of time, after all," she said, unable to keep the bitterness out of her voice. Sean didn't answer; his eyes were locked onto the screen of his laptop, his brow furrowed in concentration.

"Sean?" she asked, intrigued by his intense focus. "What are you looking at?"

"Remember the second man I spotted in the parking lot?" Sean asked without looking up. "His name is Caleb Johnson. He's a commercial fisherman, late thirties, rugged-looking guy with a salt-and-pepper beard. He's got a passion for fly fishing in his spare time, and there are plenty of pictures of him fishing around the Ember River."

Peyton leaned over to catch a glimpse of Caleb's social media profile on Sean's screen. There were indeed numerous photos of him standing knee-deep in the river, proudly holding up his catches with an infectious grin. Despite her disappointment regarding Samuel Prescott, she couldn't help but feel a spark of hope reignite within her.

"Could he be our guy?" Peyton asked, trying not to get her hopes up too high yet.

"Maybe," Sean replied cautiously. "But we'll need more than just a fishing hobby to connect him to the murders."

"Let's try calling him," Peyton suggested, her eyes fixed on the screen displaying Caleb Johnson's social media profile. The thought of potentially being one step closer to finding Julia Raimi's attacker sent a shiver down her spine.

"Good idea," Sean agreed, pulling out his phone. He dialed the number listed on Caleb's profile, and they both waited with bated breath for an answer. As the phone rang, the tension in the small office room seemed to thicken, each ring feeling like an eternity.

"Come on, pick up," Peyton muttered under her breath, her fingers tapping nervously against the desk. She glanced out the window at the sunlight that cast a warm glow over the park, wondering where Caleb might be at this very moment.

But there was no answer. The call went to voicemail, leaving them both empty-handed and frustrated. Sean hung up without leaving a message, his eyebrows furrowing in annoyance.

"Damn it," he muttered, turning back to his laptop. "Maybe we can find something else on his page that might give us more to work with."

As they continued scrolling through Caleb's photos and posts, Sean suddenly stopped and leaned closer to the screen, his eyes narrowing at something that caught his attention. "Wait a second," he said, almost whispering. "Look at this."

Peyton moved closer to see what had piqued his interest. It was a photo of Caleb standing by a tree near the Ember River, grinning as he held up a large fish. But it wasn't the fish that had drawn Sean's gaze—it was the tattoo on Caleb's forearm. A distinctive design of intertwined vines and leaves encircled his arm, partially obscured by the rolled-up sleeve of his shirt.

"Those vines," Peyton murmured, her heart starting to race. "Could that be the tattoo Julia was talking about?"

"I think it's time we brought Julia in on this," Sean said. "Ask her if this is the guy."

Peyton nodded, writing out a quick text message with the picture attached. She sent it to Julia, then sat back, hoping they wouldn't have to wait long.

Sean drummed his fingers on the table. Julia tapped her foot, willing Julia to see the message.

"Come on, come on," Peyton murmured.

Then her phone chimed, and Peyton practically leaped forward. She picked the phone up and stared at the message on the screen.

"What's it say?" Sean asked, leaning closer.

"One word," Peyton said as her pulse quickened. "'YES.'"

CHAPTER FOURTEEN

"Are you sure Caleb is supposed to be here today?" Peyton asked, her gaze scanning the area around them. They stood on a wooden dock along the Ember River, the water's surface reflecting the afternoon sun.

"Positive," Sean replied. "I talked to a few locals, and they all said he comes here like clockwork. Not much variation in his tours."

The Great Smoky Mountains National Park spread out around them, a breathtaking display of nature's beauty. The Ember River flowed gently through the landscape, its waters teeming with fish that darted beneath the surface. Along its banks, the dense forest boasted an array of trees draped in vibrant foliage—reds, oranges, and yellows clinging to their branches. The air was crisp and carried the earthy scent of fallen leaves, damp soil, and the faint aroma of pine.

As Peyton stared upriver, she couldn't help but worry. What if they were wrong about Caleb Johnson's whereabouts? What if he'd somehow found out they were looking for him? She didn't want to blow this opportunity, which was why they were still wearing plainclothes rather than switching back into uniforms. They needed to talk to him, find out if he was the man who'd attacked Julia Raimi. If they spooked him, they might lose their only lead.

Peyton continued to watch the river, lost in thought. If Caleb Johnson didn't show up, what would their next move be? She ran her fingers through her dark hair, trying to come up with a plan. They couldn't afford to waste any more time on dead ends. Not when there was a killer out there who had already claimed two lives—and apparently tried to take a third.

"Look, there," Sean said suddenly, his blue eyes narrowing as he pointed upriver. Peyton followed his gaze and saw a boat coming around a bend in the river. It was a sizable tour boat, painted forest green with a white canopy shielding the passengers from the sun. As it drew nearer, the gentle hum of its motor filled the air.

Aboard the boat were a dozen or so tourists, their faces alight with excitement and curiosity. But it was the guide who caught Peyton's attention. Standing at the helm, clad in khaki shorts and a matching shirt, was a man she presumed to be Caleb Johnson. He was in his late thirties, rugged-looking with a salt-and-pepper beard that framed his strong jawline. A tattoo snaked up his right forearm, visible even from a distance.

That's him, alright, she thought.

As the boat approached, Peyton could hear the guide addressing his passengers. "I hope you've all enjoyed your tour of the Ember River. As we make our way back to the dock, keep an eye out for any last-minute wildlife sightings—the great blue herons love this time of day."

The guide expertly maneuvered the vessel alongside the wooden platform, cutting the engine as the boat glided into place. With practiced ease, he secured it to the dock using thick ropes looped around weathered posts. The boat itself was well-maintained, each detail – from the polished brass fixtures to the neatly coiled ropes – speaking to a sense of pride in its upkeep.

"Thank you all for joining me today," the guide called out as he finished tying the boat down. "I hope you take home some amazing memories of your time on the Ember River." His voice was warm and inviting, a stark contrast to the tension that knotted in Peyton's stomach.

As she watched him interact with his passengers, she couldn't help but wonder: Could this man really be connected to the attempted drowning of Julia Raimi? Was he capable of something so sinister?

The passengers disembarked from the tour boat one by one, their faces flushed with excitement and awe. They chattered animatedly amongst themselves as they walked toward the nearby parking lot. A middle-aged couple, the woman clutching a camera around her neck, exchanged stories of the wildlife they'd spotted during the tour. A family of four, their young children tugging at their parents' hands, eagerly recounted the twists and turns of the river, their eyes wide with wonder.

Meanwhile, the guide – whom Peyton presumed to be Caleb Johnson – busied himself with securing the boat. He coiled ropes with practiced ease, his strong hands moving deftly over the worn fibers.

Peyton and Sean approached the guide together. As they drew closer, he looked up, his face breaking into a broad, cheerful grin. "Hello, there! Interested in booking a tour?"

"Are you Caleb Johnson?" Sean asked, skipping any pleasantries. The man's smile vanished, replaced with a guarded expression that set off alarm bells in Peyton's head. "Why do you want to know?" he replied, his voice suddenly wary.

"We'd like to talk to you about an incident that happened on this river," Peyton explained, trying to keep her tone even and non-threatening. "A near-drowning." Caleb's eyes narrowed, and he turned his attention back to the boat, feigning ignorance. "I don't know what you're talking about."

Sean was not deterred. He pulled out his badge, holding it up for Caleb to see. "We're park rangers," he said, "and we believe you might have information that could help us in our investigation."

Caleb scoffed, deliberately ignoring the badge and continuing to fuss with the boat.

"Look," Sean said, "we're not here to cause any trouble. We just need to talk to you about a serious matter."

Caleb shot Sean an icy stare, his jaw set in a firm line. "I've got nothing to say," he growled. "Now leave me the hell alone. I'm sick of being harassed by people like you."

Peyton sensed Caleb's anger simmering just beneath the surface, and she knew she needed to approach the situation carefully. She stepped forward, her voice gentle but firm. "Mr. Johnson, we're not here to harass you. We just want to talk. We're just trying to learn the truth."

"Right, you 'just want to talk,'" Caleb parroted sarcastically, rolling his eyes as he continued to work on the boat. His hands moved with quick, jerky motions, betraying his agitation. "That's what they all say. You people are always trying to ruin me, but I won't let you." He sounded paranoid, his voice taking on a desperate edge.

"We're not trying to ruin you. We're just trying to get information. If you haven't done anything wrong, then there's no reason for you to be worried."

"Ha! Easy for you to say," Caleb retorted, bitterness thick in his voice. "You don't have the cops breathing down your neck every damn day."

As Caleb finished securing the boat, he made a sudden move to walk along the dock toward the shore. Sean, however, quickly stepped in his way, blocking his path. Caleb's face flushed with frustration, and he demanded, "Get out of my way!"

Sean held his ground, his eyes unwavering as they stared into Caleb's. "You really should talk to us. She might have survived, but it was still attempted murder."

"Murder?" Caleb scoffed, his laugh hollow and full of disbelief. His eyes darted away, as if he was considering his options. Peyton could practically see the gears turning in his head.

Then, in a heartbeat, everything changed. With a sudden burst of strength and anger, Caleb shoved Sean hard, sending him tumbling into the water. Peyton's breath caught in her throat as she watched her partner splash into the river, taken completely by surprise. Wasting no time, Caleb raced along the dock, his escape now his only priority.

As Sean surfaced, gasping for air, Peyton knew she had to act quickly. She sprinted after Caleb, her heart pounding in her chest with each step. The world around her narrowed to a laser focus on the fleeing man, the sounds of the river and the rustling leaves fading into the background.

The dock seemed to stretch out endlessly before her, but Peyton was determined not to let Caleb escape. Her muscles burned with effort, but she pushed herself even harder, knowing that this might be their only chance to uncover the truth.

At the end of the dock was a small parking lot where a number of the tour guests were getting into their vehicles. Caleb sprinted across the lot, his salt-and-pepper beard whipping against his face. Peyton's heart thundered in her chest as she followed suit, her eyes locked on him. The sun glinted off the windshields of the parked cars, momentarily blinding her, but she didn't slow down.

"Stop running!" Peyton shouted, her voice strained with effort. She hoped that something in her tone would reach through to him, convince him that they weren't the enemy. But Caleb only looked back at her with wild, panicked eyes, and then pushed himself harder, weaving between the parked cars with surprising agility.

The smell of exhaust filled Peyton's nostrils, and the sound of her own labored breathing filled her ears.

Caleb glanced over his shoulder one more time, his expression a mixture of fear and determination. It was clear that he would do anything it took to escape their grasp, even if it meant putting himself in harm's way.

And just as this thought crossed Peyton's mind, a car pulled out of its parking spot without warning. Caleb had no time to react—he collided with the side of the moving vehicle, his body crumpling against it before he fell to the ground, groaning in pain.

"Stay in your car," Peyton called to the driver, an elderly woman who had started to climb out of her seat. Peyton turned her attention back on Caleb as she approached him cautiously. He lay on the asphalt, his face contorted in pain.

"Put your hands behind your back," Peyton said, reaching for her handcuffs. Caleb hesitated, his eyes darting to the side as if considering trying to get away again.

"Don't even think about it," she said. "You won't make it three steps."

Before he could respond, she grabbed his arm and pulled it behind his back. He winced as she secured the cuffs around his wrists, the metal clinking against itself as it locked into place.

"Peyton!" Sean called out, soaked from head to toe as he stumbled toward them, water dripping from his clothes and hair. "You got him?"

"Got him," Peyton said, breathing heavily. She could feel the adrenaline beginning to ebb away.

"Nice work," Sean said, his gaze settling on Caleb with a mixture of anger and disappointment. "You know, Caleb, if you'd just talked to us, we might have been able to help you. Now look where you've ended up. All we wanted was the truth."

Caleb's only response was a low, bitter laugh. "You want the truth? The truth is I wish she did die, considering all the trouble she's put me through. How's that?"

CHAPTER FIFTEEN

Peyton's gaze dropped to Caleb Johnson's feet, studying his footwear. The boat shoes he wore were made of high-quality leather, their tan hue softened by age and use. Their soles were designed for traction on wet surfaces, perfect for someone who spent their days around water.

But they weren't moccasins. Peyton couldn't shake the nagging thought that perhaps Caleb had simply chosen a different pair of shoes today; it didn't necessarily mean he was innocent or incapable of being Julia Raimi's attacker.

She, Sean, and Caleb were in a cramped, windowless room at the park's headquarters. The walls were a sterile off-white, decorated only by a faded poster outlining wilderness safety rules. A single fluorescent light fixture buzzed overhead, casting harsh shadows and amplifying the tension in the air. It wasn't an ideal environment for interrogation, but it would have to do.

Caleb Johnson sat slumped on the chair, a rugged-looking man in his late thirties with a salt-and-pepper beard and an air of defiance. The bruises from his headlong collision with the vehicle were starting to darken on his forehead and cheek, but he still managed to keep a steely gaze fixed on Peyton and Sean. His posture might have been that of defeat, but his eyes held no surrender.

"Look, Caleb," Sean said, having changed into dry clothes after his unexpected swim in the river. "Staying silent isn't going to help you. If you wanted us to believe you're innocent, you shouldn't have run away from us." Caleb's expression remained sullen and unyielding as he stared at the two investigators.

Peyton, her intuition tugging at her, decided to take a different approach. "Earlier, you mentioned something about the police breathing down your neck," she said. "Could you clarify what you meant?"

Caleb's eyes flicked to her, narrowing in disbelief, as if she was asking the most obvious question in the world. "You really need me to spell it out for you, huh? It's because of the incident. The woman nearly drowned, and I got blamed for it. But it wasn't my fault. I swear, I'm innocent."

Peyton could sense Sean bristling beside her, preparing to challenge Caleb's words. It wouldn't help their cause to antagonize the man further, though, so she quickly stepped in before the situation escalated.

"Okay," she said, her voice steady and calm. "Why don't you tell us your side of the story? Help us understand what happened."

For a moment, Caleb seemed to consider her request, his eyes searching hers for any hint of insincerity. Finally, he took a deep breath and let it out slowly, his eyes fixed on a point beyond Peyton. "We were on a stretch of the Ember River where the current is particularly strong," he began. "I warned everyone on the tour about the dangers of that part of the river. Most people listened, but there was one woman who didn't seem to care."

Peyton could almost see the scene unfolding before her as Caleb continued. The group of tourists stood near the water's edge, the sound of rushing water filling their ears. The sun dappled through the trees surrounding the river, casting a warm golden light onto the scene.

"Despite my warnings," Caleb said, his voice grim, "this woman started taking selfies close to the riverbank. She was standing on a slippery rock, trying to get the perfect angle. I told her again to step back, but she just laughed me off." He paused, shaking his head at the memory. "Next thing I knew, she lost her footing and fell into the water."

Peyton could picture the woman's scream, followed by the sickening splash as she hit the water. The relentless current would have dragged her under in an instant, leaving only ripples behind.

"Everyone panicked, but I managed to keep my head," Caleb continued. "I grabbed a long branch and extended it to her, telling her to hold on with all her might. It took the help of the other guests, but we eventually managed to pull her out of the river, drenched and terrified. She survived, but just barely."

He sighed again. "Once the paramedics took her away, I figured that would be the end of it. But she went to the police and started saying all sorts of things about me. Claimed that I didn't warn her properly about the dangers of the river."

As Peyton listened to Caleb's story, a sense of unease settled over her. What did this have to do with Julia Raimi?

Caleb ran a hand through his hair, his face contorted with indignation. "But she was flat-out lying. I warned all of them repeatedly about the dangers of the river and how strong the current could be. But she just had to get that selfie."

Peyton studied Caleb's face, searching for any hint of deception. She had developed a keen eye for liars during her time with the FBI, but Caleb seemed genuinely upset and bewildered by the whole ordeal.

"Ever since then, the police have been breathing down my neck, harassing me like I tried to murder her or something," he continued. "When I saw you two coming after me, I thought you were just more cops looking to make my life miserable."

Peyton exchanged a glance with Sean, who looked as puzzled as she felt. They had come to question Caleb about Julia Raimi, not some other woman who had nearly drowned in the Ember River. What was going on here?

"What does this have to do with Julia?" Sean asked, voicing Peyton's thoughts.

"Julia?" Caleb frowned. "No, that wasn't her name. I think it was Heather something."

"Julia Raimi," Peyton said. "Does that name mean anything to you?"

Caleb shook his head. "Should it?"

Peyton's heart sank. Was this all a grand waste of time, a colossal misunderstanding?

"She was attacked and nearly drowned in the Ember River three months ago," Sean said. "We believe the person who tried to drown her may be responsible for the deaths of two other women in the area."

Caleb's eyes widened with horror. "I swear, I don't know anything about that. The only incident I know of is the one I just told you about." He looked back and forth between the two of them. "Is that why I'm here? You think I'm some kind of serial killer?"

"Let's get back to the shoes," Sean interjected, his tone serious. "Do you own a pair of moccasins?"

Caleb looked confused by the question but nodded. "Yes, I have a pair of moccasins. But what does that have to do with anything?"

"Could you describe them for us?" Peyton asked.

"Actually," Caleb said hesitantly, "I have a better idea. If you let me use my phone, I can show you a picture of them."

Peyton and Sean exchanged glances again before Sean gave a curt nod. He excused himself and left the room to retrieve Caleb's phone, leaving Peyton alone with the suspect. The silence between them was heavy, and she couldn't help but feel torn—was Caleb playing a part, or did he genuinely believe they'd brought him here to discuss an entirely different matter? She studied his face, searching for any sign of deception, but found none.

The sound of a door opening snapped Peyton back to the present as Sean returned, Caleb's phone in hand. "Here," he said, handing the device over to its owner. Under Sean's watchful eye, Caleb unlocked the screen and began scrolling through his gallery.

"Here it is," Caleb said finally, offering the phone to Peyton and Sean so they could see the picture he'd found.

In the photo, Caleb stood beside a roaring campfire, the flames casting an orange glow on his rugged features. He wore a pair of brown leather shoes that, at first glance, appeared to be moccasins. However, upon closer inspection, subtle differences in the design became apparent. The stitching was more intricate, and the soles seemed sturdier than the soft, supple material Julia had described. They were clearly not the same shoes.

Peyton's heart sank as she realized they had no concrete evidence to link Caleb to the crimes. Her fingers tightened around the edge of the phone as she handed it back to him, disappointment churning in the pit of her stomach. She glanced at Sean, who seemed to share her frustration, his jaw clenched and eyes narrowed.

Still reeling from the realization that Caleb Johnson wasn't wearing the shoes Julia had described, Peyton decided she couldn't let him go without making sure he was truly innocent. She needed to be thorough in her investigation, for both Amanda Torres' and Kimberly Saunders' sake.

"Mr. Johnson," she began carefully, "I appreciate your cooperation so far. Can you tell us where you were this morning?"

Caleb hesitated briefly. "I met up with a group of fellow fishermen at a local diner for breakfast, then we all took a trip to the marina. We were there for hours, discussing boat maintenance and repairs."

"We'll need the names of the other fishermen," Sean said.

"Of course."

As he spoke, Peyton could see the sincerity in his eyes, and it became apparent to her that there was no way he could have been near the river during the time of the attack, despite the fact that Julia had identified him. Unfortunately, such misidentification wasn't uncommon.

"Thank you for your honesty," she said quietly. "We don't have any reason to hold you any longer. You're free to go."

"Listen, I understand you're just doing your job," Caleb replied, his voice softer than before. "Good luck finding whoever killed those women." With that, he left the room, leaving Peyton and Sean to process the information they'd gathered.

"Where do we go from here?" Peyton asked as she turned to Sean, feeling the weight of disappointment settle heavily on her shoulders.

"Back to square one, I suppose," Sean replied, rubbing his temple in frustration. "We'll have to find another lead."

Just as they were about to discuss their next move, Sean's phone rang, cutting through the tense atmosphere like a knife. He answered the call, and as he listened, Peyton could see his face becoming increasingly grave. The furrow in his brow deepened, and his eyes took on a distant, troubled look.

"Who is it?" Peyton whispered anxiously when Sean finally hung up, unable to contain her curiosity any longer.

"Another abduction," he said, his voice strained with concern. "A young woman was taken from a campsite in the park. Looks like our killer isn't slowing down."

CHAPTER SIXTEEN

"Chloe seemed totally normal," Caden Anderson said, his voice strained with worry. "I have no idea what happened."

Peyton couldn't help but study Caden, Chloe Garcia's boyfriend, as they walked through the campground. He was tall and lean, with light brown hair that hung just past his ears, brushing against the collar of his denim jacket. His eyes were a piercing blue, but any warmth they might have held was overshadowed by the shadows beneath them, hinting at sleepless nights and unspoken worries.

Caden seemed nervous, his fingers fidgeting with the hem of his jacket as he spoke. Peyton sensed something unhealthy about his relationship with Chloe, an unease that went beyond the concern of a worried boyfriend. She could see it in the way he avoided meeting their gaze, his words coming out in hurried bursts as if he were trying to convince himself of their truth.

They were making their way across Whispering Pines Retreat, the campground Chloe had been staying at, toward a trail in the woods where, according to Caden, Chloe had claimed to be going shortly before she disappeared. Around them, the campground was silent except for the soft murmurs of conversation as rangers questioned other campers, their faces knit together with shared worry.

"Chloe and I...we've had our problems," Caden went on. "But I never thought anything like this would happen."

Peyton couldn't shake the feeling that there was more to their relationship than Caden was willing to admit. She wondered what secrets lay under the surface, hidden behind his carefully constructed facade.

Sean turned to Caden, his face somber and serious. "What were you and Chloe doing here in the park?"

Caden hesitated for a moment before answering. "We just wanted to spend some quality time together, away from the city," he explained, his words slow and measured. "I convinced her to come out here, even though she's not really into camping. I thought it'd be good for us, you know? A chance to reconnect and unwind. Even bought us a pair of matching bracelets—you know, so everyone would know we were a pair."

He let out a short laugh, but the sound was hollow and forced like he was trying too hard to make light of the situation. Peyton couldn't help but feel that Caden was manipulating the conversation, steering it in a direction that would cast him in a more favorable light. His eyes darted around as he spoke, avoiding both hers and Sean's gaze, and she could see the gears turning in his mind, calculating each word he uttered.

"Chloe wasn't too keen on the idea of camping at first," he continued with a wry smile. "She's more of a city girl, you know? But I managed to persuade her. Told her it'd be an adventure, something we could look back on and laugh about someday."

The way he made light of Chloe's reluctance seemed disingenuous, as if he was downplaying her concerns to make himself seem more agreeable. Peyton could almost hear the unspoken words lingering in the air between them, the subtle insinuations that Chloe had been the one standing in the way of their happiness, and not him.

They reached the trail leading into the woods, the path marked by a simple wooden signpost bearing the name 'Sprucewood Trail'. The trail itself was narrow and winding, flanked on either side by towering, ancient trees that seemed to almost lean in over the path, casting dappled shadows on the ground below. The aroma of damp soil and decaying leaves filled the air, marking the change of seasons with every breath.

"Last time I saw Chloe, she said she was going for a run along this trail," Caden told them, his voice cracking slightly as he spoke. "She wanted to get some exercise, clear her head. I didn't think twice about it."

"Did you see anyone else talking to Chloe before she went for her run?" Peyton asked, her eyes scanning their surroundings, searching for any signs of disturbance or struggle.

Caden shook his head. "No, but I wasn't really paying attention. I got caught up talking to some other campers and lost track of time. I should've been keeping an eye on her, making sure she was okay." His words were tinged with regret, but underneath it all, Peyton could sense a hint of possessiveness, as if he believed he had the right to control Chloe's every move.

"Thanks for your help, Caden," she said, giving him a tight-lipped smile. "Just remember not to leave the campground, alright? We might have more questions for you later."

Caden nodded, his eyes downcast as he walked away from them. As soon as he was out of earshot, Sean turned to Peyton, his brow furrowed. "What do you think? Do you believe his story?"

Peyton hesitated, her gaze lingering on Caden's retreating figure. "I'm not sure. He seems manipulative, and there's something unnerving about how controlling he appears to be when it comes to Chloe."

"Agreed," Sean said, rubbing his chin thoughtfully. "Do you think it's possible he kidnapped her?"

"Maybe, but you'd think someone else would've noticed," Peyton pointed out. "It's hard to imagine he could've taken her without anyone seeing."

"True," Sean said, his eyes scanning the area around them. "Still, we should keep an eye on him just in case."

With that settled, they set off along the trail, which was blanketed in a lush carpet of green grass. The path wound its way through the forest, flanked by towering trees whose branches reached out like gnarled fingers, casting dappled shadows on the ground below.

"Where do you think Chloe is now?" Sean asked, his voice low as if he were afraid the trees themselves might be listening.

"Based on the killer's MO, I think he's probably taking her to the Ember River to drown her, like he did with the others," Peyton replied, her heart heavy at the thought of what Chloe must be going through. "We can only hope one of those search teams we sent that way will intercept them."

Sean glanced over at her, his blue eyes filled with concern. "It's a long river," he said. "There's no telling where the killer might take her."

"All the more reason to focus on finding clues here," Peyton said. "We can't let another woman die because we weren't able to piece things together in time."

Her eyes scanned the ground as they walked along the grassy trail. Then she spotted something.

"Look," she said, stopping in her tracks. Her gaze had locked onto a patch of mud near the edge of the trail. A pair of golf cart tracks were imprinted into the soft earth, cutting through the otherwise pristine landscape. Her stomach twisted into knots as she imagined the killer following Chloe in a golf cart, closing in on his prey.

"Damn," Sean muttered, his expression grim as he crouched down to examine the tracks more closely. "This means he could be anywhere by now."

As they continued walking, Sean pointed out a set of footprints in another patch of mud. They were small and more delicate, undoubtedly belonging to Chloe. Based on the footprints' spacing, it appeared as though she had been jogging. Or was she running from the killer?

"She must've known something was wrong," Peyton said. "She was trying to escape."

Sean nodded, his jaw clenched. "We need to find her before it's too late."

They followed the trail, their eyes peeled for any further signs of Chloe or the killer. Soon, they came across a place where the grass was torn up, suggesting that the golf cart had come to an abrupt stop. Peyton searched for Chloe's tracks but found nothing.

"Over here," Sean called out, gesturing to a set of footprints leading off the path and into the woods. They were partially hidden beneath a layer of fallen leaves, but once spotted, their direction was unmistakable.

"Good catch," Peyton said, her pulse quickening as they ventured off the trail. The farther they strayed from the path, the more treacherous the terrain became, with tangled roots and slippery moss threatening to trip them up at every turn.

"Stay close," Sean said as they pushed through the underbrush, their clothing snagging on thorny vines that seemed to reach for them like desperate fingers. "There's no telling what we might find."

Peyton's mind raced as she tried to piece together what had happened to Chloe. Had she managed to elude the killer for a time, only to be caught later? Or was she still out there somewhere, running for her life?

The thought spurred her forward, her senses heightened as she scanned the ground for any clue that might lead them closer to the truth.

As they moved deeper into the woods, the once-friendly forest seemed to morph into something sinister, a ravenous beast eager to swallow them whole. Amidst the heavy silence, only the rustling of leaves beneath their feet and the distant calls of birds could be heard.

Eventually, they stumbled upon an area that looked as though it had been the stage for a violent struggle. The foliage was trampled, and broken branches littered the ground. A torn piece of fabric, possibly from Chloe's clothing, clung to a nearby bush.

"Looks like this is where the killer caught up with her," Sean said grimly, examining the scene with a trained eye. "I think they fought here, and then he dragged her back to his golf cart and took off."

Peyton nodded, her heart sinking at the thought of Chloe's terror during the altercation.

As she continued scouring the area, Peyton noticed something glinting in the underbrush—a small, silver charm bracelet half-buried amongst the leaves. She picked it up, turning it over in her hands. It was adorned with tiny charms shaped like hearts, stars, and even a miniature camping tent. She showed it to Sean, who frowned.

"That must be the bracelet Caden mentioned," he said. "Chloe probably dropped it during her struggle with the killer. Doesn't do us any good, though—she's probably halfway to the river by now."

"The question is," Peyton said, gazing through the forest as she imagined the long, winding river making its way through the vast wilderness, "which part of the river?"

CHAPTER SEVENTEEN

"Alright, so we've got about fifty carts here," Rufus, a greenskeeper on the golf course, said as he ran a hand through his short-cropped salt-and-pepper hair. "They're used mainly by park employees for maintenance and transportation within the park, but on occasion, some visitors borrow them too. We keep track of them through a digital system. Each cart has a unique ID number, and when it's checked out, the employee or visitor's name is logged alongside it."

Peyton listened intently, her dark eyes scanning the rows of golf carts as she considered the possibilities. Could the killer have used one of these to abduct Chloe Garcia? She studied the layout of the barn, noting its position in relation to the campground where Chloe had been taken. It wasn't far—close enough for someone familiar with the area to navigate easily between the two locations.

"Does anyone ever have trouble returning the carts?" Sean asked, his lean face expressionless as he scrutinized the vehicles.

"Sometimes," Rufus admitted. "People forget or get sidetracked. But we usually find the missing ones before too long."

Peyton's brow furrowed as she contemplated the implications. What if the killer had employed multiple carts, stealing one and then returning it before anyone grew suspicious? It would explain how he'd managed to avoid detection thus far. The golf carts were quiet, unobtrusive, and perfect for navigating the park's narrow paths.

"Have any carts gone missing recently?" she asked.

Rufus scratched his beard thoughtfully. "I'd have to check the system, but I think we've had a couple go missing over the past few weeks. They usually turn up eventually, though."

"Could you get us a list of the missing carts and their last known locations?" Sean asked.

"I don't really have access to that information," he said, rubbing the back of his neck. "Even if I did, I wouldn't have the authority to share it with you."

"Who would have access to that kind of information?" Peyton asked.

"Well, my supervisor, Peter Billings, might know more. He oversees the whole operation."

"Where can we find him?"

"He should be in his office at the main visitor center," Rufus replied, gesturing toward a large building in the distance.

"Thank you," Peyton said with a polite smile before motioning for Sean to follow her. They headed outside, making a beeline for the visitor center. Sean was quiet, reserved.

"What are you thinking?" Peyton asked, studying her partner as he ambled beside her. He had an easy gait that spoke of years traversing the wilderness, and he kept his eyes up, scanning his surroundings for danger.

"I'm thinking that this killer is smart," Sean said, his voice low. "Using golf carts to move around the park is a smart way to avoid detection. It's quiet and inconspicuous."

Peyton nodded. "But it also means that he knows the park well. He knows which paths to take and which areas to avoid."

"Exactly," Sean replied. "And that means we need to tread carefully. We don't want to spook him."

That was the very thing Peyton feared—spooking the killer without knowing it. The trail would go cold, and he might disappear forever. Or he might pop back up in another park to kill again, and it might take years for anyone to make the connection between the two cases.

They reached the visitor center, and Sean – gentleman that he was – held the door for Peyton. She entered, followed by her partner, and found herself in a large lobby filled with people. Families with children, couples holding hands, and elderly visitors all milled about, browsing the various exhibits and displays. Peyton scanned the room, searching for any sign of Peter Billings. She finally spotted him across the room, standing behind a desk and talking to a young woman.

"Excuse me," Peyton said, approaching the desk. "Are you Peter Billings?"

Billings turned to face her, his eyes narrowing. "Who's asking?"

"Ranger Peyton Risk," she said, flashing her badge. "This is my partner, Sean O'Malley. We're here investigating the abduction of Chloe Garcia."

Billings nodded, his expression softening slightly. "Yes, I've heard about that. What can I do for you?"

"We understand that there have been a few golf carts that have gone missing recently," Peyton said. "We were hoping to get a list of those carts and their last known locations."

Peter hesitated, pressing his lips together. "Look, I don't want to get involved in all this," he said, shaking his head. "I've got enough on my plate without having to deal with an investigation."

"This isn't just a kidnapping," Sean said, keeping his voice low so that others wouldn't hear. "We believe the man who kidnapped Ms. Garcia has killed at least two others and attacked a third."

Peter's face paled. "Let's go into my office, shall we? No sense causing a panic."

Peyton and Sean followed Peter into his office, a spacious room with a large wooden desk and a window that overlooked the park. The walls were adorned with pictures of various animals and landscapes, and there was a comfortable-looking leather armchair in one corner. A monitor stood in the center of the desk.

"Please, have a seat," Peter said, gesturing toward a pair of chairs in front of his desk. Peyton and Sean sat down, and Peter took his own seat behind the desk. He looked tired, Peyton noted, dark circles under his eyes, and lines etched deep into his forehead.

"I understand that you're investigating a serious crime," he began, his voice low. "But I don't want to get anyone in trouble without just cause. Those carts go missing quite often, and it doesn't mean there's anything sinister behind it."

Peyton studied him for a moment, observing his body language and searching for any clues that might indicate what could change his mind. She noticed a picture frame on his desk, showcasing a photograph of Peter with his family – wife, two kids, and even a golden retriever – all smiling happily in front of a camping tent.

"Peter, your family seems to enjoy the park as well. We're trying to keep everyone safe here, including them," she said softly, pointing to the picture. "We need your help to catch this killer before he causes any more harm. What would you do if the missing woman was *your* daughter?"

Peter looked at the picture, then back at Peyton. His expression softened, and he sighed, relenting. "Alright," he conceded. "I'll see what I can do. You don't have to lay a guilt trip on me."

He turned on the computer, logged in, and began typing away. "We set up an app to keep track of the golf carts," he said. "It's not perfect, but at least it gives us some idea what's going on." He scrolled, then stopped abruptly and tapped the mouse. "These are the ones we can't account for."

"Can you send me that information?" Peyton asked, pulling out her phone.

"Sure," Peter agreed, taking down her number and sending her a screenshot of the list. "I hope it helps."

Peyton's eyes widened as she studied the list of missing golf carts on her phone. The sheer number of unaccounted-for carts was staggering, and she couldn't help but feel a pang of anxiety in her chest. Each one of these could potentially be the vehicle the killer was using to move around the park undetected. She glanced over at Sean, who was scrutinizing the list with equal intensity.

"Can you believe how many are missing?" Peyton murmured, biting her lip as she scrolled through the digital record. "It's like looking for a needle in a haystack."

Sean nodded, his blue eyes narrowing in thought. "This definitely just got more complicated."

The killer had been able to abduct and murder multiple victims without being caught, which suggested an intimate knowledge of the park's layout and resources. If he was indeed using stolen golf carts, it meant he had some way of accessing them without raising suspicions.

"Now," Peter said, rising, "if you'll excuse me..."

He was halfway to the door when Peyton called to him. "Wait a minute! Is there any way you could find out *who* borrowed these missing carts? Are there any records of that?"

Peter hesitated, his shoulders tensing as he considered her request. He seemed to weigh the consequences in his mind before finally speaking. "I...I suppose I could look up the names of the people who borrowed them," he admitted reluctantly. "We do have a digital record of that information."

"Could you please check it for us?" Peyton pressed, her dark eyes pleading with him. "It could be the breakthrough we need to solve this case."

Peter sighed, clearly conflicted. But as he looked into Peyton's determined gaze, something within him seemed to shift. Whatever reservations he had about getting involved in the investigation were overshadowed by his desire to help bring the killer to justice.

"Alright," he agreed, returning to the computer once more and navigating through the app that tracked the golf carts. "Let me see if I can find what you're looking for."

With a few clicks, Peter located the list of names associated with the missing golf carts. He scrolled through it briefly, his brow furrowed in concentration, before sending the list to Peyton. As soon as her phone buzzed with the incoming message, she couldn't help but feel a surge of anticipation.

"Is there anything else you need from me?" he asked, clearly frustrated by the extent of his involvement in the investigation. His voice held a tinge of impatience, and it was clear that he felt out of his depth.

"No, thank you," Peyton replied, offering him a genuine smile. "You've been a great help."

Peter nodded and left them alone in the office, the hum of fluorescent lights overhead punctuating the silence between Peyton and Sean.

As Peter disappeared into the lobby, Peyton pulled up the list of names on her phone. Beside her, Sean leaned in, his eyes scanning the screen intently. The list of names, like the list of missing carts, was long, and it quickly became evident to Peyton that they would need to work together to cross-reference it with the park's visitor records, searching for any potential connections or suspicious individuals.

"Alright," Sean said decisively, breaking the silence. "Let's split up the list and start checking these names against the park's visitors. We need to see if any of them stand out or have any connection to the victims."

"But how are we going to figure out the visitor list?"

Sean grinned. Rising from the chair, he moved around to the other side of the desk and sat down in front of the computer. He raised his hands in a gesture of helplessness. "It's not my fault he left his computer logged in," he said.

CHAPTER EIGHTEEN

Chloe's eyes fluttered open, her vision blurry and unfocused. Her head pounded, and a sickly taste lingered in her mouth. As she tried to move, she realized that her hands were tied behind her back with rough rope, digging into her wrists. Her ankles were bound together as well, the same abrasive material biting into her skin.

"Where...where am I?" Chloe mumbled, struggling to make sense of her surroundings. She was lying down, her body sprawled across the hard metal floor of a golf cart.

As panic rose in her chest, she tried to piece together what had happened. Images flashed through her mind—a hiking trail, the sun sparkling through the trees in Great Smoky Mountains National Park. A man driving a golf cart followed her as she walked, his voice a constant buzz in her ears.

"Hey there, need a lift?" he'd called out, grinning at her from beneath his baseball cap. She remembered feeling uneasy at the sight of the man's greasy, intent smile. She'd politely declined and continued walking, hoping he would leave her alone.

But he hadn't. He'd kept talking, kept following, and when she'd broken into a jog, he'd only accelerated.

Chloe recalled the moment she couldn't take it any longer. Fear gripped her like a vice, and she sprinted into the woods, desperate to escape the stranger. He pursued her on foot, his heavy breathing loud behind her as she raced through the undergrowth. Then everything went dark, his hands wrapping around her throat, squeezing the air from her lungs until she lost consciousness.

Now she found herself trussed up like an animal, her pulse galloping as she struggled to free herself. Tears filled Chloe's eyes as the reality of her situation set in. She couldn't believe this was happening to her. As she tried to make sense of it all, her thoughts turned to Caden, her boyfriend.

The man who attacked her had tried to convince her to break up with him. But why? Did this stranger have some sort of vendetta against Caden?

Is Caden involved in all of this? she wondered. Caden was certainly a bit rough around the edges, and sometimes his pranks went too far, but surely he'd never do something this wild.

She wiped her tears with her shoulder, knowing that crying wouldn't help her now. She needed to pull herself together if she wanted any chance of escaping. Straining her neck, Chloe studied the sky above her, noting the position of the sun. It hadn't been long since her attack—maybe an hour or two at most.

So where was her attacker?

Taking a deep breath, Chloe mustered the courage to sit up and assess her surroundings. She found herself on a dirt trail, flanked by towering trees that cast dappled shadows across the ground. A dense understory of shrubs and ferns created a natural wall on either side of the path, making it difficult for her to see beyond their green curtain.

Above the rustling leaves, a faint but persistent rushing sound reached her ears. Water? Was she near a river or a stream? If she could somehow reach it, maybe she could follow it to safety, or at least find someone to help her.

"Okay, Chloe," she whispered to herself, attempting to quell her rising panic. "You can do this."

She wiggled her wrists, trying to loosen the ropes that bound her hands behind her back. With each twist and turn, she felt the rough fibers digging into her skin, but she refused to let the pain deter her. She had to get free.

"Come on," she muttered, frustration mounting as the ropes refused to give way. "Just a little more..."

Regardless of how much she struggled, however, she could not loosen the ropes. All at once, it occurred to her that it was far more important to escape her abductor than to escape her restraints.

Taking a deep breath, Chloe wiped away her tears and scanned her surroundings again. She had to find a place to hide, somewhere the man wouldn't think to look for her. Her eyes landed on a cluster of thick bushes not far from where she was, their dense foliage providing a dark contrast against the surrounding trees. The branches twisted and tangled together, forming a natural barrier that seemed impenetrable.

Maybe, Chloe thought, *if I can get behind those bushes, he won't be able to find me.*

Chloe took a deep breath, bracing herself for the pain she knew would come when she pushed her bruised and battered body over the side of the golf cart. She started by kicking her legs over the side. Then she wormed the rest of her body over, until suddenly she landed hard on the unforgiving earth, the impact knocking the wind out of her.

For a moment, all she could do was lie there, gasping for air as stars danced before her eyes. Panic clawed at her throat; she was terrified that the man would suddenly appear and drag her back to the golf cart.

Please, no, she thought, her heart pounding in her chest. *Not now, not when I'm so close.*

But as the minutes ticked by, there was no sign of him. The only sound Chloe could hear was the rhythmic rush of water in the distance, growing louder with each passing moment.

She began crawling.

Inch by agonizing inch, Chloe dragged herself toward the thick bushes that promised her safety. The leaves had turned shades of golden yellow and fiery red in the early winter months, their vibrant colors giving her a small sense of hope amidst her fear. She grimaced with each movement, her muscles protesting the strain they were under, but she knew she couldn't afford to stop.

Keep going, she urged herself, the mantra repeating in her thoughts like a chant to ward off danger. *You can do this.*

The thought of spending the night on the cold, hard ground was far from appealing, especially for someone who had always taken pride in her city-girl lifestyle. But now, the prospect of a rough night in the wilderness seemed like a small price to pay if it meant escaping the clutches of that maniac.

As she finally reached the protection of the bushes, Chloe felt her heart starting to slow down. She nestled herself deeper into their embrace, hiding her body behind the twisted branches and thick foliage. From here, she could cautiously peek out at the golf cart that had once been her prison, waiting for the man to return.

Please, let him think I ran away, she prayed silently, watching the sun dip lower in the sky. Darkness would soon fall over the forest, cloaking her in shadows and making it even more difficult for him to find her.

The rustle of leaves and snapping of twigs behind her sent a jolt of fear coursing through her veins.

Probably just a squirrel, she told herself, trying to keep her breathing steady. She glanced over her shoulder but saw nothing out of the ordinary. For a moment, she allowed herself to believe that maybe, just maybe, she had successfully evaded her captor.

But then the underbrush stirred again, and this time, there was no denying the figure emerging from the trees. The man's eyes locked onto hers, and despite the distance between them, the cold fury burning within their depths was unmistakable.

"No!" she screamed, desperation giving her voice a raw, ragged edge. She scrambled away on her hands and knees, her fingers clawing at the dirt and leaves as if they could somehow propel her to safety. But it was no use—he caught up with her easily, his footsteps heavy and deliberate as he closed the gap between them.

"Did you really think you could get away from me?" he sneered, grabbing her by the arm and hauling her to her feet. "How foolish."

With one swift motion, he picked her up as if she were nothing more than a bag of trash, tossing her unceremoniously into the back of the golf cart. Chloe whimpered, tears streaming down her face as she stared up at him, terror clawing at her insides like a living thing.

"Please," she said. "What are you going to do with me?"

"Be quiet and listen," he commanded, his tone cold and unyielding. She swallowed hard, her throat tight with fear, and obeyed.

"Tell me," he said after a moment of silence, his voice dripping with menace. "What do you hear?"

Chloe strained to pick out any sound beyond the frantic beating of her own heart. "I don't hear anything."

"Wrong answer. Listen more carefully."

She did. Then it occurred to her what he was talking about.

"The river," she said.

"That's not the river," he said, a smile spreading across his face like a stain. "*That* is the sound of your destiny."

CHAPTER NINETEEN

"I'm gonna be honest," Sean said, leaning back in his chair, "I'm worried what might happen to Chloe while we're wading through this list of names."

Peyton took a deep breath, wanting to argue but knowing her partner had a point. They were sitting at a small table for two in a quaint restaurant located in Elkmont Historic District. The rustic charm of the eatery was complemented by the warm glow of antique lamps hanging from the ceiling. Exposed brick walls, adorned with vintage photographs, hinted at the area's storied past.

Outside, visible through a window at Peyton's elbow, the historic district showcased a collection of buildings that had once been at the heart of a thriving logging community. Peyton couldn't help but feel a sense of nostalgia as she took in the sight of the well-preserved structures. These remnants of a bygone era stood as silent witnesses to the lives of the people who had once called this place home. She found herself drawn to the stories that lay hidden beneath the weathered timber facades, wondering what the lives of earlier generations had been like here.

Peyton and Sean had spent the last hour sifting through the names given to them by Peter Billings, looking up the identities of each member on the list and cross-referencing them against criminal records, social media profiles, and news articles to determine if any had a violent history or suspicious tendencies. They had also tried to establish alibis for each person during the time of the murders, reaching out to their contacts in local law enforcement and searching online for any potential clues.

Despite their meticulous efforts, however, they had yet to find anything promising. Each name seemed like a dead end, leaving them no closer to identifying the killer than when they started.

"Maybe we need a different approach," Peyton suggested, her fingers drumming against the table, which was laden with the remains of their dinner: scattered French fries, hamburger buns, and a few lonely pickle slices. Her laptop was there, too, the keys slick with grease.

"There has to be something we're missing," she added.

Sean rubbed his temples in frustration. "Whatever it is, we need to find it soon. We have no idea how much longer Chloe has—assuming she's still alive."

Peyton took a moment to look around the room, hoping to find some inspiration or a fresh perspective on their case. As her eyes scanned the room, they settled on a familiar face sitting at the bar.

Saul? she thought, puzzled.

Yes, it was indeed Saul Guzman, her former foster father. He was tall, with salt-and-pepper hair and a strong build. His kind eyes crinkled at the corners as he noticed her, his face lighting up with genuine happiness.

"Peyton!" he called out, his voice booming with enthusiasm as he made his way toward their table. "What a pleasant surprise!"

"Hey, Saul!" Peyton said, standing up and embracing him in a warm hug. "It's so good to see you." She turned to her partner. "Sean, this is Saul Guzman. Saul, meet Sean O'Malley, my partner at the NPS."

"Nice to meet you, Sean," Saul said, extending his hand for a firm handshake. "I've heard a lot about you from Peyton."

"Likewise," Sean replied, his usual stoicism giving way to a slight smile.

"What brings you here?" Peyton asked, curious about the unexpected encounter.

"I was actually in the area for a conference on sustainable forestry practices," he explained.

"Okay," Peyton said slowly. "But how did you know *I* would be here? It's not like I live here—my job takes me all over the country."

Saul chuckled, his eyes twinkling with mischief. "Well, I happen to know some friends in your department, and I may or may not ask about you now and then, just to see how you're doing."

"And you couldn't just ask me?" Peyton asked, raising an eyebrow in amusement.

"I know how you like to paint a rosy picture, make me think everything's going well. Sometimes I like to hear the truth from a less biased source."

"By spying on me."

Saul shrugged unapologetically. "What can I say? I love my daughter."

Peyton smiled, feeling a sense of warmth and comfort wash over her. She loved that Saul referred to her as his daughter. He had never treated her like she was adopted, never acted like she was anything other than his own flesh and blood.

"Anyway," he continued, "when I heard you were here, I couldn't pass up the chance to reconnect. It's been far too long."

Peyton agreed wholeheartedly, feeling an overwhelming sense of comfort and familiarity in his presence. It had indeed been too long since she'd seen him last, and it felt like a small blessing amidst the pressure of their investigation.

"Please, join us," Sean said, gesturing to an empty chair at their small wooden table.

"Thanks," Saul said, taking a seat and glancing at the fries on Peyton's plate. "You gonna eat those?"

"Go right ahead," Peyton replied, pushing the plate toward him.

It felt strange for her to see Saul and Sean together, as she usually kept her professional life separate from her personal one. The reason for this was twofold: firstly, she believed it helped maintain her focus and objectivity while working on cases; and secondly, the traumatic events of her past – the death of her parents, as well as the ups and downs of the foster system – had left her wary of letting people get too close. She knew that mixing these aspects of her life would only lead to complications and vulnerability—something she couldn't afford in her line of work.

Despite these reservations, however, Peyton found herself enjoying the company of both men. Sean and Saul, though from vastly different backgrounds, seemed to get along well and share a mutual respect for one another.

"So, Peyton," Saul said, wiping his hands on a napkin after devouring the last of the fries. "What brings you to this neck of the woods?"

"A case," Peyton said. "Big surprise, right?"

Saul leaned toward Sean, speaking conspiratorially. "Peyton has always had a strong sense of justice," he said, smiling warmly at her. "I knew she'd be successful in whatever field she chose."

Sean nodded. "She's one of the best investigators I've worked with," he said, glancing at Peyton with a small smile.

Peyton felt a rush of pride and gratitude at their words, feeling a renewed sense of motivation for their case.

"So," Saul asked, "what's this case about?" His eyes flicked between Peyton and Sean.

"Well," Peyton began cautiously, "I can't give away too many details, but I can share the basics." She hesitated for a moment before continuing. "There's been a series of drownings in the area, and we believe they've all been perpetrated by the same person."

Saul's eyebrows shot up in surprise, but he nodded, encouraging her to go on.

"We've got a list of potential suspects," she explained. "The problem is, it could take hours to sort through all these suspects. Meanwhile, a young woman is missing, abducted presumably by the killer."

"Sounds challenging," Saul mused, rubbing his chin thoughtfully. "Where exactly have these drownings taken place? Are they in different bodies of water, or—"

"All in the same river," Peyton said.

"Ah." Saul leaned back and frowned at the table. "Maybe the killer has some kind of connection to the river, then. Maybe he grew up nearby, or he has some emotional attachment to it."

"Or he's just using it to destroy any DNA he might have left," Sean said.

Saul nodded. "That's possible, too." He took a deep breath and let it out slowly as he checked his watch. "Well, I'm no detective, so I won't try to do your thinking for you. But I'm sure you two will figure it out." He pushed back his chair and rose.

"Are you leaving already?" Peyton asked, disappointed.

"I promised a friend I'd meet him for dinner," Saul said. "He just lost his wife and he's going through a lot, so I don't want to miss the opportunity to be there for him. I'd stay longer if I could." He put an arm around Peyton and hugged her.

"I know you would," Peyton said as she hugged him back. "Well, it was good seeing you for a few minutes, at least."

He smiled. "You, too, kid." Then he turned to Sean and extended his hand. "Look out for her, will you?" he asked, shaking Sean's hand.

"Do my best," Sean said.

Saul nodded, satisfied, and walked off. Peyton watched him leave the restaurant, a pang of nostalgia and gratitude lingering in her heart.

"Seems like a good guy," Sean said, sipping from his coffee cup.

"More than you know, Sean," she replied. As Saul disappeared from sight, Peyton sank back down into her seat, disappointed.

"Was that helpful?" Sean asked.

She sighed. "Not really. We need to focus on this list of names, need to figure out if the killer is one of these people. If we change things up now, try a different approach—"

She stopped suddenly, her gaze falling on her open laptop and the list of names there, including all the information she'd managed to compile on each suspect so far. One of the occupations was listed as 'water quality specialist.' That got her thinking.

"Peyton?" Sean asked, concern etched across his face as he observed her sudden intensity. "What is it?"

"The river, Sean," she said, her eyes lighting up with excitement. "Like Saul said, there's a good chance the killer has some kind of connection with the river. What if his job connects him to the river?"

Sean sat up straighter, looking thoughtful. "It's worth a shot."

As Peyton scanned the information on her laptop, she noticed a number of water-related jobs: lifeguards, swimming instructors, fishing guides, and so on.

"Check this out," she said, pointing at the screen. "These people all have jobs that involve water. They would be comfortable in the water, good swimmers."

Sean furrowed his brow, staring intently at the names Peyton had highlighted. "Interesting," he said. "But how do we know which one of them is the killer? We can't just go around accusing people without solid evidence."

"Then we need to narrow down the list to those who've spent extensive time in the park."

"How do we do that?"

"By checking for any park permits or fishing licenses that might've been issued to them," she said. "We can also investigate where these people live in relation to the river, how much free time their jobs allow. Even if we can't establish a motive yet, if we can figure out who'd have the ability to commit the killings..." She trailed off, losing herself in her work.

As she worked her way through the list, she managed to cut down the group to a few dozen. Then she began ruling out people based on their alibis: those who were out of town during the drownings, or who had credible witnesses vouching for their whereabouts. As she crossed off name after name, she felt a mixture of relief and frustration: relief that these people were innocent, and frustration that the killer was still out there, hidden among the remaining suspects.

And then, she saw him: Ed Davis, a lifeguard at a local swimming pool. He stood out from the rest of the names not only because of his job but also because of his striking appearance—tall, muscular, with short-cropped blonde hair and eyes as blue as the water he spent his days guarding. Something about him seemed to resonate with Peyton, making her think back to her conversation with Julia Raimi.

"Sean," she said slowly, her voice tinged with uncertainty. "Remember what Julia said about the man who attacked her? That he called himself 'Guy' and kept insisting that he was 'saving her' even as he tried to drown her?"

"What about him?" Sean asked.

"Take a look at this," Peyton said, turning the laptop screen toward Sean. "Ed Davis. Lifeguard at a local swimming pool."

Sean leaned in for a closer look at the screen, his eyes scanning over the information on Ed Davis. His eyebrows pulled together. "Well, that's interesting."

"Maybe, in his own twisted way," Peyton said, "he is putting the victims in danger so he can act out trying to save them. But he ultimately kills them because he can't have witnesses."

"Are you saying you think the killer has a savior complex?"

Peyton nodded. "And who better to have one," she asked, "than a lifeguard?"

CHAPTER TWENTY

The first thing that caught Peyton's eye was the intricate pattern of dried mud tracks in the driveway. They seemed to crisscross and weave like a spider's web. She crouched down, her dark hair framing her face as she examined the impressions.

They were at the house of Ed Davis, the lifeguard who had borrowed one of the golf course's carts and failed to return it. To this point, they had no incriminating evidence against him, but his profession – a job that revolved around water – suggested to Peyton that he was worth looking into.

Not to mention the fact that his home was located within a few miles of the Ember River.

"Look at the tire treads," she said to Sean, who was standing beside her. "Do you think they match the pattern we found near the crime scene?"

Sean frowned, his eyes narrowing as he opened his phone and compared the tracks to the pictures he had taken earlier. "It's hard to say for sure, but the width and tread pattern seem consistent with a golf cart."

"Could he have driven here on the golf cart from the park?" Peyton wondered aloud, looking up at the house and then back at the muddy tracks. "Maybe he brought his victims here before drowning them."

Sean straightened up, considering her words. "It's possible. The location is remote enough that no one would notice anything unusual happening here."

Peyton stood up, her suspicions growing stronger. The house's proximity to the park made it an ideal spot for someone trying to go unnoticed. And being a lifeguard, Ed Davis would have the necessary knowledge and skills to drown his victims without drowning himself.

Just then, the door to Davis's house creaked open, and an overweight, elderly woman stepped out onto the porch. Her gray hair was pulled back in a tight bun, and her piercing hazel eyes were framed by deep wrinkles. She wore a faded floral dress that had seen better days, and her thick arms were crossed over her chest as she scowled at Peyton and Sean.

"Who are you two? And what are you doing snooping around in my driveway?" she demanded, her voice stern.

"Hello, ma'am," Peyton began, taken aback by the woman's sudden appearance. "Are you Ed Davis's mother?"

"Who wants to know?" the woman replied, narrowing her eyes suspiciously.

"Ma'am, we're with the National Park Service," Sean said, holding up his badge for her to see. "We're investigating a series of incidents that occurred in the park, and we believe your son might have some information that could help us."

"Ed?" Mrs. Davis scoffed, shaking her head. "I don't know where he is. I can never keep track of him these days. He might be in the house, or he might be off somewhere else. Who knows?"

"Would it be possible for us to come in and have a look around, just in case he's here?" Sean asked politely, giving her a reassuring smile.

Mrs. Davis hesitated, glancing between them uncertainly. "I don't know about that..."

"Please, Mrs. Davis," Peyton interjected earnestly, trying to appeal to the maternal instinct she hoped the woman still possessed. "We really need to speak with Ed. It's important, and we don't mean Ed any harm. The sooner he speaks with us, the sooner we'll be out of his hair—and yours."

The elderly woman studied them for a moment longer before finally relenting. "Alright, but make it quick," she warned, opening the door wider to let them in. "This isn't a motel."

Stepping inside the house, Peyton was immediately struck by the distinct smell of animals. The interior was dim and cluttered, with worn furniture and knickknacks adorning every available surface. Family photos lined the walls, telling the story of Ed's life from childhood on into adulthood.

As they moved farther into the living room, Sean nudged Peyton and nodded toward the corner where an old tabby cat curled up on a plush armchair, watching them intently with its green eyes. A large golden retriever dozed on a dog bed nearby, while a parrot perched high on a stand, eyeing the new visitors warily.

"Beautiful animals you have here, Mrs. Davis," Peyton said, smiling at the elderly woman as she reached down to give the dog a friendly scratch behind its ears. The dog wagged its tail in response, letting out a contented sigh.

"Thank you," Mrs. Davis replied, her demeanor softening ever so slightly. "They're good company."

"Ed!" she suddenly bellowed, making Peyton jump. Mrs. Davis began to move through the house, her voice rumbling through the rooms as she called for her son. "Ed! You got visitors!"

Silence greeted her calls, and Peyton exchanged a glance with Sean. Where was Ed? Was he back at the park?

"Mrs. Davis, when was the last time you saw your son?" she asked.

"Last night," the woman replied with a sigh. "He came home late, mumbling something about needing to get some things done before heading out again. It's not unusual for him to disappear for hours on end, but he always comes back eventually."

Peyton's intuition told her that there was more to this story than met the eye. Ed's late-night activities and his mother's lack of knowledge about his whereabouts set off alarm bells in her mind.

"Is there any place he might have gone? Anywhere you think we should check?" Peyton pressed, hoping to glean some useful information from the woman.

Mrs. Davis thought for a moment, her brow furrowing. "Well, he sometimes hangs out at the park or goes hiking in the mountains. But I really couldn't say for sure where he'd be right now."

"Does he have any friends he likes to spend time with?" Sean asked. "Anyone you can think of who might know where he is?"

"Ed's always been a bit of a loner," the woman replied hesitantly. "He has some acquaintances from work, but I don't really know them. He doesn't talk much—not to me, anyway."

Peyton cleared her throat. "Excuse me, Mrs. Davis. Do you mind if I use your bathroom?"

"Of course," Mrs. Davis said. "Just down the hall. The one with the toilet in it." There was a flicker of amusement in her eyes.

Peyton caught Sean's eye and subtly nodded her head toward Mrs. Davis, silently urging him to continue engaging her in conversation. She wanted to explore the house further, hoping to find some clue as to Ed's location or any evidence linking him to the murders.

As Peyton moved away, Sean took a quick breath, the kind that signaled a shift in the conversation, and asked Mrs. Davis, "So it's just the two of you here?"

Mrs. Davis nodded. "That's right—well, us and the pets. The dog, his name is Trooper. Ed's father named him that years ago, on account of..."

Peyton tuned them out. The hallway she had entered was narrow, the wallpaper peeling slightly at the edges. Family photos adorned the walls, capturing moments of joy and laughter long past. As Peyton passed each one, she couldn't help but feel a pang of sympathy for Mrs. Davis—living with someone she hardly knew, yet bound by familial ties.

She counted the doors along the corridor, including the bathroom, and stopped at the third one on the left. Judging by the hippie poster on the door, she guessed this was Ed's room. Turning the doorknob slowly, she pushed the door open and stepped inside.

The bedroom was surprisingly neat, with a meticulously made bed and carefully organized shelves lined with books on wilderness survival and local flora and fauna. A hiking backpack hung from a hook on the wall, and a collection of camping gear was neatly stowed in the corner. The room seemed to reflect a person who took pride in their independence and resourcefulness.

Peyton's eyes were drawn to a corkboard pinned with maps and photos of the surrounding park areas. There were notes scribbled in the margins detailing various routes and points of interest. It was clear that Ed had an intimate knowledge of the landscape, and Peyton felt a growing sense of unease as she considered the implications.

As she continued her search, Peyton heard Sean's voice drifting down the hallway, skillfully keeping Mrs. Davis occupied with questions about Ed's hobbies and interests. She knew she didn't have much time before the woman realized she was missing and began to ask questions. With renewed urgency, Peyton began rifling through drawers and closets, trying to find anything that might lead them closer to the truth.

As she carefully examined the shelves, her attention was drawn to several items—a compass, a hunting knife, and a collection of primitive fire-starting tools. These were not just everyday camping essentials; they were tools designed for survival in harsh conditions. She couldn't help but wonder if Ed had used these skills to facilitate the crimes he was suspected of committing.

She continued her search, and her heart skipped a beat when she found a worn leather journal tucked between two books. Pulling it out, she hesitated for a moment before opening it, feeling like she was violating someone's innermost thoughts. But she needed answers, and any clue could be vital.

The pages were filled with detailed notes on various hiking trails, weather patterns, and wildlife observations. Flipping through them, she noticed that most entries were dated, making it easy to track Ed's outdoor activities. She paused abruptly when she reached a more recent entry, written early that morning.

"Shimmering Peaks," she read aloud, her voice barely above a whisper. "There's a cave near the ridge. Perfect spot for some solitude. I'll camp there tonight."

Peyton's heart raced at the discovery. *Gotcha,* she thought, closing the journal. She was about to leave the room when something caught her eye—a small gap between the wall and the dresser. Curious, she moved closer and discovered that something had been wedged into the narrow space. She reached in, her fingers brushing against soft fabric.

As she pulled it out, she realized that it was a sneaker—a woman's sneaker, seemingly forgotten or deliberately hidden. The size was far too small for either Ed or his mother.

So whose sneaker was it? Chloe's, or one of the other victims'?

CHAPTER TWENTY ONE

The sun dipped low in the sky as Peyton and Sean navigated their ATVs through the treacherous terrain of Great Smoky Mountains National Park. The ground was a chaotic mix of jagged rocks, fallen branches, and steep inclines, making it difficult for the vehicles to find purchase.

Shimmering Peaks, the location Ed Davis mentioned in his journal, was remote, with no direct roads leading to it. It was clear that whoever chose this place as a hideout wanted to remain hidden.

As they neared Shimmering Peaks, the landscape shifted dramatically. Lush foliage gave way to exposed rock faces, which gleamed in the fading light like an ancient fortress. The Ember River meandered nearby, deceptively swift. They dismounted their ATVs and looked around.

"I don't see any caves," Sean said, his voice tinged with frustration. "Are we sure we're in the right place?"

Peyton studied the mountainside herself, searching for any indication of hidden crevices or entrances. But she found nothing. Doubt wormed its way into her thoughts, her stomach churning at the possibility that she had misunderstood the journal entry.

She tried to recall a conversation she'd had with her father years ago. They had been hiking together in Eden's Gate National Park when he had shared his knowledge of geography and cave formations with young Peyton. She remembered him saying something about certain geological features that could hint at the presence of hidden caves.

"Water," she muttered, the memory bubbling to the surface. "Dad said that caves often form near water sources because the flow erodes the rock over time."

It was not a particularly surprising fact, but the reminder was helpful now. If her father's advice held true, there was a strong possibility that a cave could be hidden somewhere near the Ember River. With renewed determination, Peyton focused on the steep slopes that rose around them, searching for any signs of a hidden entrance.

"Where are you going?" Sean asked as he noticed Peyton start to climb one of the steeper slopes, her hands grasping at rocks and roots for support.

"Caves are often found near water sources," she said. "We should check the slopes around the river."

Sean nodded and followed suit, scaling the incline with practiced ease. They ascended higher and higher until they reached the top of the ridge, their calves burning and lungs gasping for air. As they stood side by side, catching their breath, Peyton felt a surge of gratitude for her father's wisdom. His love for the outdoors and his desire to share it with her had provided her with invaluable skills, skills that might just lead them to the answers they sought.

"Look!" Sean exclaimed suddenly, pointing to the opposite slope. There, nestled between craggy rocks and shadowed by gnarled trees, was the mouth of a cave.

"Looks like your dad knew what he was talking about," he added.

The cave's entrance was partially obscured by a thick curtain of hanging vines, making it nearly invisible to the untrained eye. Its dark maw seemed to beckon them, promising secrets hidden within its depths.

As they carefully picked their way down the slope, a sense of foreboding weighed heavy on Peyton's chest. Could this cave be Ed Davis's hideout? Did he use it as a base to sneak out and drown his victims?

Peyton kept her hand close to her holster, ready to draw it at a moment's notice. She and Sean moved cautiously forward, stepping over gnarled roots and loose rocks that threatened to trip them up.

"Look," she whispered, pointing at faint tracks leading to the cave entrance. They appeared to be fresh, likely made by someone coming or going recently.

"Could be Ed's," Sean murmured, studying the prints. "Let's proceed with caution. We don't know what we're walking into."

As they reached the cave entrance, the strong odor of marijuana hit them like a wave. It was unmistakable, seeping out from the darkness within. Peyton hesitated for a moment, then switched on the flashlight on her phone, casting a feeble light into the dim interior.

"Ed?" she called cautiously.

"Who's there?" came a groggy reply, followed by a figure stirring in the back of the cave. The man crouched low, lifting a hand to shield his bloodshot eyes from the sudden light. He looked disheveled, with unkempt hair and clothes that hung off his frame.

"Ed Davis?" Peyton asked.

"Y-yeah…that's me," he admitted, sounding dazed and confused. His slurred speech and unfocused gaze made it clear he was high. This surprised Peyton. Then again, it could be his way of coping with the guilt of his crimes.

"How long have you been out here?" Peyton asked.

"A few hours," Ed replied, his gaze unfocused and his words slow. "I like to come out here and relax, clear my head. It's just me and nature, y'know?"

Peyton nodded. Inwardly, though, she thought that 'clearing his head' was the opposite of what he was doing. She scanned the interior of the cave, wondering if Ed had a weapon. They needed to get him out into the light, where they could speak with him on their terms.

"Do you mind coming out for a minute so we can talk to you?" she asked.

Ed shook his head. "Can't do that, sorry. I like it in here. But you're welcome to join me if you want. It's cozy." He laughed.

Peyton and Sean exchanged a glance.

"I'm not going in there," Sean said in a low voice. Peyton wasn't interested in entering the narrow cave, either. They would just have to question Ed from where they were.

"We spoke with your mother," Peyton began.

"Yeah?" Ed's voice sounded far away, uninterested.

"I saw the sneaker in your room," she continued. "The one hidden between your dresser and the wall."

Ed blinked at her, looking puzzled. "You went into my room?" His eyes widened, a flicker of clarity cutting through the haze. What was it that flashed in his eyes? Anger?

"Whose shoe is it, Ed?" Sean asked. "We know it's not yours."

Ed sighed, rubbing his forehead as if trying to piece together a puzzle. "I found it on a trail a few days ago. I thought maybe someone had lost it and would come back for it. So, I picked it up, intending to return it if I ever came across the owner."

Peyton didn't believe him. She had come across plenty of stalkers and serial killers who collected souvenirs from the victims who caught their attention. Whether or not this man was a killer, she doubted he'd intended to return the sneaker.

"Then why did you hide it in your room?" she asked.

Ed was silent for several heartbeats. "I didn't want my mom to find it. I knew she'd be suspicious, think I was up to no good."

"Now why would she think that?" Sean asked.

Ed's eyes darted around, avoiding theirs. "I don't know. Maybe because of the drownings?"

Peyton and Sean exchanged a look.

"What do you know about the drownings?" Peyton asked.

Ed shrugged. "Nothing much. Just rumors."

"What rumors?" Sean asked.

"That there's someone going around, drowning women in the Ember. A serial killer, I guess." His eyes suddenly cleared. "Is that why you two are here? You think I'm somehow involved?"

"That's what we're trying to figure out," Peyton said, studying him carefully. Could this really be their guy? Could someone looking so unkempt and smelling so strongly of weed make his way around the park without anyone remembering him?

Then something obvious occurred to Peyton—she hadn't seen any vehicles around.

"How did you get out here, Ed?" she asked.

"Drove out on my dirt bike," he said.

"Not your golf cart?" Sean asked.

Ed scratched his scruffy beard. "I lost that one—think someone stole it."

"Where did it go missing?" Peyton asked. Was he being honest, or was this just his way of throwing them off the scent?"

"Over by…um, it was Settlers' Gully, I think." He sounded a bit uncertain.

"What were you doing there?" Sean asked.

"I was just riding around, looking for some new trails to explore," Ed replied, his eyes unfocused again. "I like to head out and get lost for a while. It's peaceful."

Peyton and Sean exchanged another look. Peyton could tell Sean was just as uncertain what to make of Ed as she was.

"Why not just take your bike?" Peyton asked.

Ed shrugged one shoulder. "It's loud, and sometimes the rangers get on my case about driving through the park. That's why I borrowed one of the carts—much quieter. I'm probably screwed now, though, because I lost it. With my luck, they'll probably make me pay for it."

"Can we take a look at your bike?" Peyton asked. She needed to see the bike with her own eyes to confirm he wasn't lying to them.

Ed hesitated for a moment, then nodded. "Sure. It's parked over by those trees." He pointed to a cluster of trees at the edge of the clearing.

"Stay here with him," Peyton said to Sean in a low voice. "I'll go take a look."

Sean nodded, his eyes never leaving Ed's face. Peyton set off toward the trees, walking carefully around the edges of the clearing. As she reached the trees, she could see a flash of metal amongst the undergrowth. She moved closer and saw the dirt bike, a sleek black machine with a powerful engine. It looked muddy, but otherwise well-cared-for.

Satisfied, she headed back to the cave. Sean raised his eyebrows expectantly when he saw her, and Peyton motioned for him to join her so they could talk where Ed wouldn't hear them.

"Looks like he might be telling the truth about the golf cart," Peyton said. "Or he just hid it somewhere."

Sean nodded. "One way or another, we need to find it. If he's telling the truth and he did in fact lose the cart, it's possible the killer stole it."

"I was thinking the same thing."

"But we can't just let Ed go," Sean said. "He had our vic's shoe in his room, for goodness' sake."

Peyton nodded solemnly. "Then we'll just have to split up. You stay here, see if you can't coax him out of that cave, and I'll head over to Settlers' Gully."

"You sure?" Sean looked doubtful. "You don't even know the way."

"Good thing I came prepared."

Peyton pulled out a map from her backpack, spreading it across the rocky ground. She had already marked the locations where the four victims had been attacked, and now she circled Settlers' Gully. She stared at the map, surprised.

"I'll be damned," Sean said, echoing her thoughts. "It's right in the middle of it all."

Peyton nodded, more convinced by the second that they were close to a breakthrough. "And if we can find the golf cart tracks there, they might lead us straight to the killer."

CHAPTER TWENTY TWO

Peyton was leaning over the handlebars of the ATV, gazing intently ahead as the wind whipped her chestnut hair out behind her, when suddenly a large black shape loomed in front of her.

Shit!

Peyton slammed on the brakes, skidding to a stop just inches from the creature.

It was a black bear, massive and imposing, its brown eyes locking onto hers with an unnerving intensity. Its fur was matted and damp, giving off an earthy scent that mingled with the crisp night air. The bear's breaths came out in visible puffs, and it stood there motionless, as if challenging her right to be on the trail.

"Easy, big fella," Peyton whispered under her breath, trying to keep her voice steady. She didn't want to make any sudden movements that might provoke the bear.

After what felt like an eternity, the bear finally grunted and ambled off into the brush, disappearing from sight. Peyton exhaled slowly, realizing how close she had come to colliding with the animal. If she hadn't stopped in time, the impact could have killed both her and the bear.

As the bear disappeared, Peyton resumed driving. She gripped the handlebars tightly, determined to reach Settlers' Gully as quickly as possible without risking another dangerous encounter. The ATV roared beneath her, its powerful engine eating up the distance as she navigated through Tennessee's Great Smoky Mountains National Park.

Peyton didn't like splitting up at a time like this, but it was too risky to let Ed Davis go free. *I just hope Sean's able to find a way to rule Ed out soon, Peyton* thought. *I could really use his help searching out here.* She had called in a search helicopter to look for the missing golf cart. There was no telling how soon it would arrive, however, and in the meantime she was on her own.

The forest around her was a mix of dense foliage and towering trees, their branches reaching out like gnarled fingers against the dark sky. As Peyton sped through the forest, her keen eyes scanned the area for any signs or markers that could lead her to Settlers' Gully.

Suddenly, she spotted a wooden signpost up ahead, illuminated by the ATV's headlights. Braking hard, she skidded to a stop and squinted at the weathered text.

"Settlers' Gully," she read aloud, relief flooding her system. She glanced around, noting how the landscape had changed. Steep, rocky walls rose up on either side, framing the narrow passage like a giant, ominous corridor. Shifting her gaze upward, she saw the silhouettes of birds perched on jagged outcroppings, silent observers to her mission.

Finally, she thought, her heart pounding in her chest. *Now I just need to find that damn golf cart.*

She dismounted the ATV, her boots crunching on the damp earth as she let out a quiet sigh. Settlers' Gully was eerily silent; only the distant hooting of an owl broke through the stillness. She took a moment to steady her nerves before pulling out her phone and activating the flashlight feature.

She moved cautiously along the trail, sweeping the beam of light across the ground as her eyes searched for tracks. Around her, on either side, clusters of ferns and small saplings rose up from the forest floor. The occasional gnarled tree trunk loomed over her like some crude Halloween prop.

As she pushed farther into the gully, she noticed faint impressions in the soft soil, evidence of previous hikers who had ventured off the main path. It gave her a slight sense of comfort knowing that others had traversed this area, though their reasons for doing so remained a mystery.

"Think like the killer, Peyton," she urged herself, taking a deep breath. "What would he do with a stolen golf cart?"

It occurred to her that a golf cart wouldn't be able to navigate this terrain very well. There had to be another road nearby, something broader, with more space from the encroaching wilderness. She hadn't noticed any such roads so far, but then again, she hadn't really been looking for such roads, either.

Determined, she retraced her steps back to the ATV. Climbing into the driver's seat, she allowed herself a moment to collect her thoughts. Then, with a renewed sense of purpose, she started the engine and began to drive slowly through the gully, her eyes peeled for any sign of an access road.

"Come on," she whispered, frustration evident in her voice. "Where are you hiding?"

Each bump and jolt along the rough terrain sent a shudder through her body. As the seconds ticked by without any sign of a road, however, she began to wonder if she had already passed it. Should she double back? Or would that only waste more time?

Just as her hope began to wane, she caught sight of a wide opening between the dense trees. An access road. Relief washed over her.

Now let's find those tracks, she thought, turning the ATV onto the road and driving slowly, her eyes peeled for any signs of disturbance on the ground.

After only a short distance, she spotted what she was looking for: the now-familiar pattern of a golf cart's tires. They were unmistakable: the parallel lines left by the wheels, the distinctive tread pattern, and the shallow indentations in the soft ground. This was definitely a golf cart's trail, and she had no doubt they been made by the cart Ed Davis borrowed—considering how remote this area was, it seemed highly unlikely others would drive carts out here.

"Gotcha," Peyton murmured, excitement bubbling up inside her.

As she followed the tracks, her heart raced faster, and she became more and more convinced that she was closing in on the killer. The question was, did he have Chloe Garcia? Or had he drowned her already?

Just then, the road split. The area was too grassy for her to tell which way the cart had gone, so she stopped the ATV and got off, crouching to study the ground. Before she could draw any conclusions, she was startled by the sound of a man's laughter from the trail ahead.

What the hell? she thought.

Hurriedly, she turned off the ATV and listened intently. She didn't hear the laughter again, but that was alright. She knew which branch of the trail it had come from, and now there was no need to study the tracks.

Her pulse pounded in her ears as she carefully crept forward through the now-silent forest. She came around a bend, and the moon – which must've recently emerged from behind the clouds – cast a silver glow on the scene before her. A few hundred feet away, parked haphazardly at the edge of a cliff in a small clearing, was the golf cart she had been searching for, its metal frame glinting in the pale light. It looked out of place amidst the natural backdrop of the forest, a harbinger of danger and death.

"Damn," Peyton whispered to herself, taking cover behind a large tree trunk. Her eyes darted back and forth, searching for any sign of movement. This was it—she had found the killer's vehicle.

But where was the killer himself?

As if in response to her question, she suddenly became aware of two figures standing at the edge of the cliff. One was a man, tall and muscular. The other was a woman, her long hair flowing in the wind as she stood perilously close to the edge, her body tense and rigid.

And somewhere far below, Peyton could hear the restless, hungry murmur of the Ember River.

CHAPTER TWENTY THREE

Under the watchful eye of a full moon, Chloe stood trembling at the edge of a cliff, her heart pounding like the hooves of a wild stallion. The man she had come to know as "Guy" loomed menacingly before her, his piercing gaze void of any compassion.

"Please," she begged, her voice wavering with fear, "don't do this."

She studied his face, searching for some hint of humanity, but found none. His eyes were cold and unfeeling; it was as if he was utterly devoid of empathy. She couldn't believe this was happening to her.

Glancing behind her, she saw the river far below, its dark waters rushing violently against the jagged rocks. It looked like a serpent in the moonlight, slithering through the landscape with an insatiable hunger for destruction. The sight chilled her. One wrong move could send her plummeting to her death.

"You should have listened to me earlier," the man said, his voice dripping with contempt. "I tried to save you from your pathetic excuse of a relationship with that waste of space you call a boyfriend."

His words stung like a slap to her face. Why would he care about her relationship with Caden? Did she know him, and she just didn't remember him?

"Instead of being grateful," he continued, "you ran away from me like I was some creep. Do you have any idea how pathetic you are?"

"You don't know me," she said, her voice barely a whisper. "I'm stronger than you think."

The man scoffed and rolled his eyes, clearly unimpressed by her defiance. Yet for Chloe, this small act of courage ignited a spark deep within her, a flickering flame that refused to be snuffed out.

Suddenly, she came to a decision. "Alright," she began, her voice trembling yet determined. "You're right. I should leave Caden."

The man's eyes narrowed, his jaw clenched. "You're just saying that because you think it's what I want to hear."

"No, I'm not," she insisted, meeting his cold gaze. "I know how abusive Caden is and how toxic our relationship has become." She swallowed hard, forcing herself to continue. "He's always putting me down, making me feel worthless. He isolates me from my friends and family, controlling every aspect of my life."

She hesitated before adding, "Sometimes he even becomes physically violent."

The man's demeanor changed, his anger seemingly replaced by curiosity as he listened intently to Chloe's words. She could only hope that opening up about her painful reality might somehow save her life.

"Then why do you stay with him?" he asked, his voice low and emotionless.

"Because..." Chloe hesitated, searching for the right words to explain her complicated feelings. "Caden wasn't always like this. In the beginning, he was charming and caring. He made me feel special."

A distant memory surfaced, and she continued, painting a picture of their past. "We met at a charity event. He was so attentive, always making sure I had everything I needed. He remembered the smallest details about me—my favorite flower, my favorite songs. It was like a fairy tale."

She paused. The man stared at her, saying nothing, his eyes willing her to continue.

"Someone even warned me about him, but I didn't take it seriously," she went on, her voice thick with regret. "I was already so emotionally invested in our relationship. It wasn't until later that his abusive behavior started to show—the manipulation, the control, the belittling, the violence."

As she spoke, Chloe's mind raced back through the years, the memories of their love now tainted by the truth of her suffering. She realized just how much power Caden held over her, and it terrified her.

It's not entirely unlike the situation I'm in now, she thought. *Caden never tried to throw me off a cliff...but that doesn't mean I wasn't his prisoner.*

"By the time I understood what was happening, I was already trapped," she confessed, fighting back tears. "I didn't know how to leave, or if I even could."

The man studied her face for a moment, as if weighing the truth of her words. In the moonlight, his expression remained unreadable, but Chloe sensed that he was considering her story—perhaps even empathizing with her plight.

If he was capable of such a feeling, that was.

"Tell me," he said, his voice cold and unyielding, "what has changed? Why would you suddenly be willing to leave him?"

Chloe swallowed hard, feeling the weight of his question bearing down on her. She thought about the fear that had held her captive for so long, the pain she'd endured at Caden's hands, and the hopelessness that had consumed her. Then she remembered the words this man had spoken earlier, the conviction in his voice when he told her she deserved better.

"Because of you," she replied, almost surprised to discover she was telling the truth. "You helped me realize that I deserve better than the way Caden treats me. I'm ready to stand up for myself, to tell him I'm done with him."

As she spoke these words, something inside Chloe shifted. It was as if a veil had been lifted from her eyes, revealing a strength she hadn't known she possessed. She felt empowered, alive with the possibility of a future free from Caden's control. The fear that had once shackled her had been broken, leaving her with a newfound determination to reclaim her life.

"I don't have to live like this anymore," she continued, her hands curling into fists at her sides. "I can choose to break free, to stand up against the abuse and take back my life. And I will."

The man studied her for a moment, his expression inscrutable in the moonlight. Then, slowly, a smile crept across his face, and Chloe's heart leaped with hope. Had she passed his test? Would he let her go?

"You're fortunate," he said, his voice almost gentle. "You will indeed get a second chance. But you'll have to fight for it. Are you ready to fight?"

Chloe nodded, the fire of resolve burning brightly within her. "I'm ready," she whispered, her body tensed like a coiled spring.

"Good," he replied, his eyes taking on a predatory gleam. Then, without warning, he lunged forward and shoved Chloe.

Chloe acted on instinct, clinging to the man's arm even as she felt her body give ground. Her fingers dug into his flesh as she struggled to keep herself from slipping into oblivion.

"Let go!" the man snarled, his face contorted with rage. "This is for your own good!"

Chloe's mind raced, searching for a way out of this nightmare. But with every passing second, the force of gravity seemed to grow stronger, threatening to wrench her from safety and send her plummeting into the abyss.

"You say you're ready to fight," he said, spittle flying from his mouth, "but all you're doing is clinging to the past! It's time for you to let go and face your future!"

As he spoke, Chloe could feel his arm beginning to slip from her grasp, the sweat on their skin making it difficult to maintain her hold. Her muscles burned with exhaustion, and she knew she couldn't hang on much longer.

But just as the last threads of hope seemed to unravel, a shout pierced the night, jolting Chloe's senses back to life.

"Leave her alone!"

Chloe turned her head, her eyes widening in disbelief as she saw a woman in a ranger's uniform emerging from the darkness. The ranger's face was set with determination, her eyes locked on the scene unfolding before her.

For the first time since her ordeal began, a spark of hope ignited within Chloe. Maybe, just maybe, she might be saved after all.

"Did you hear me?" the ranger demanded, her voice steady and commanding. "Leave her alone!"

The man hesitated for a moment, his grip on Chloe's arm faltering as he weighed his options. Then, with a chilling smile, he replied, "Fine. If that's what you want."

Before Chloe could react, the man suddenly released his grip on her arm and shoved her with all his might, sending her hurtling away from the edge of the cliff. She gasped in shock, her body twisting through the air as she fought to regain her balance.

Gravity's merciless grip tightened around Chloe as she plummeted through the frigid night air, the wind howling furiously in her ears. The cliff face raced past her, a jagged blur of stone and earth that seemed to taunt her with its cruel indifference.

And then the water struck her with a clap like thunder.

CHAPTER TWENTY FOUR

Peyton watched in horror as Chloe disappeared over the edge of the cliff, her scream piercing the cold night air as she plummeted into the darkness below. A wave of helplessness crashed over Peyton, leaving her breathless and devastated.

Was there any way Chloe could survive the fall? Could anyone?

A sinister chuckle broke through Peyton's panic, tearing her attention away from the abyss. The man, his face illuminated by the haunting moonlight, turned toward her with a cruel smile plastered on his lips. "Looks like you came just a little too late," he said.

Refusing to let fear paralyze her, Peyton raised her gun, pointing it directly at the man's chest. Her hands were steady despite the adrenaline coursing through her veins. "Show me your hands," she demanded.

The man looked down at the weapon aimed at him, seemingly unfazed. He considered her for a moment, his cold eyes boring into hers, before shaking his head slowly. "No, I don't think I'm going to do that," he said with a nonchalant shrug. "I'm going to leave now."

Peyton tightened her grip on the gun, her finger hovering over the trigger. She couldn't let this monster escape, not after everything he'd done.

"Show me your hands!" she said. "Now!"

Ignoring her words, the man began walking toward the golf cart parked nearby, each step measured and deliberate. It was as if he knew she wouldn't pull the trigger, as if he could sense her uncertainty and hesitation.

"Stop!" Peyton shouted again, her voice cracking with desperation. "I will shoot you!"

The man paused, glancing over his shoulder with a grin. "You won't shoot an unarmed man," he said. "Besides, shouldn't you be thinking about Chloe?"

Peyton's heart skipped a beat, her blood running cold as his words sank in. She could feel her resolve waver, and she hated herself for it. But what if there was still a chance to save Chloe? What if she had survived the fall into the river and was even now fighting to stay afloat as the current carried her downstream?

"Looks like you have a choice," the man continued, his voice dripping with malevolence. "You can save Chloe, or you can arrest me. It's up to you."

Peyton hesitated, torn between the urge to bring this monster to justice and the possibility of saving an innocent woman. The gun in her hand seemed to grow heavier by the second, her knuckles turning white as she gripped it.

The man called her bluff. Unhurried, he climbed into the golf cart and turned the key. Peyton aimed at him, wanting so badly to fire, but she couldn't bring herself to do it. The golf cart roared to life, the headlights illuminating the tree line.

The sound of the golf cart's engine revving broke Peyton's trance, and she dashed toward the cliff's edge, her legs pumping furiously. She couldn't stomach the thought of letting the killer escape, but Chloe's life took precedence.

As she raced toward the cliff, Peyton could hear the man's mocking laughter, quickly fading as he drove away in the golf cart. The wind whipped through her dark hair, chilling her to the bone as she pushed herself harder, faster, praying that she wasn't too late.

"Please, Chloe," she whispered under her breath, her chest heaving with exertion. "Hold on."

Moonlight glinted off the churning water below as Peyton reached the cliff's edge. The precarious drop loomed before her, a maw of darkness swallowing the jagged rocks and frothing waves. Squinting against the dim light, she searched feverishly for any sign of Chloe.

"Chloe!" she called out, her voice tight with desperation. No response came, however.

Then, amidst the chaos of the water below, something caught her eye—a glimpse of what appeared to be Chloe's head, bobbing just above the surface. But was she still alive? Peyton couldn't tell from this height, and an unsettling panic began to claw at her chest.

"Damn it," she muttered under her breath. With no other options, she knew she had to dive in. Time was running out, and finding another way down would take far too long.

Closing her eyes for a moment, Peyton drew in a deep, steadying breath. She tried to quell the fear threatening to overtake her, reminding herself that she had trained for situations just like this. Summoning every ounce of courage she could muster, she took several steps back from the edge, mentally preparing herself for the plunge into the unknown.

"Come on, Peyton. You can do this," she whispered, steeling herself for the jump.

With a final deep breath, she sprinted toward the edge, her muscles tensing as she pushed off into the void. As she fell, the wind roared in her ears, drowning out all other sounds. She felt weightless, suspended between earth and sky, her body hurtling through the darkness.

The impact with the water was jarring, a violent collision of flesh and liquid that sent shockwaves of pain through her body. The frigid water enveloped her, its icy tendrils gnawing at her skin as she sank deeper, disoriented by the sudden change in pressure.

Gasping for air, Peyton fought to orient herself, kicking towards the surface with all her might. Her limbs ached from the strain, but she pushed through it, determined to save Chloe.

As her head broke the surface, she gulped in lungfuls of air, her chest heaving from exertion and relief. Blinking away the sting of saltwater, she scanned the churning waves around her, searching for any sign of Chloe. The moonlight shimmered on the water's surface, casting an eerie glow over the ripples. At first, she saw nothing but the inky blackness of the river.

Then, as if summoned by her thoughts, she spotted a flash of color amidst the undulating waters. Squinting into the darkness, she realized that it was indeed Chloe, her body limp and facedown as the current dragged her along like a ragdoll.

Peyton swam toward Chloe with powerful strokes, trying not to believe the worst, desperately holding onto the hope that somehow Chloe might still be alive. Losing the killer was devastating, but it was a mistake they could later correct. They could follow his vehicle's tracks, or perhaps Peyton could speak with a sketch artist and try to get a detailed description of him out to law enforcement.

If Chloe drowned, however…

If only I'd been faster, Peyton thought, agonized. *If only I'd acted right away instead of hesitating...*

Finally, Peyton reached Chloe's side, her hands trembling as they grasped at the woman's soaked clothing. "Hold on, Chloe," she whispered, as much to herself as to the unconscious woman. With a Herculean effort, she began to tow Chloe's body toward the shore, fighting against the current that seemed determined to keep them both trapped in its icy grip.

When they finally reached the rocky beach, Peyton's muscles screamed in protest, but she refused to let exhaustion claim her just yet. She dragged Chloe's limp form onto the sand, turning her onto her back and checking for any signs of life.

"Come on, Chloe, don't you dare give up on me," she muttered as she tilted the woman's head back to open her airway. Placing two fingers on Chloe's neck, she searched for a pulse, praying that she would find one. The seconds stretched into an eternity.

Then, finally, she felt it—a weak, thready beat that set Peyton's own heart racing with relief.

She's alive! She's still alive!

Knowing she had no time to waste, Peyton interlocked her hands and positioned them in the center of Chloe's chest. She began performing CPR, pushing down hard and fast, the rhythm of her compressions punctuated by her own labored breathing. After thirty compressions, she pinched Chloe's nose shut and sealed her lips over Chloe's, delivering two breaths that made the woman's chest rise ever so slightly.

"Please, Chloe," she pleaded between compressions, her voice choked with emotion. "You have to fight. You can do this."

Despite her best efforts, however, Peyton felt a knot of dread tightening in her chest. What if this didn't work? What if she not only failed to catch the killer, but she failed to save Chloe as well? How would she be able to live with herself?

With one last push and a final breath, Peyton paused, praying for any sign of life from Chloe. For a few agonizing moments, there was nothing but silence—then, at last, Chloe's body convulsed, and she coughed up water, gasping for air.

"Chloe!" Peyton cried, tears streaming down her face as relief and disbelief washed over her. "You're alive!"

Chloe's voice was so faint that Peyton had to lean closer to hear her. "What…what happened?"

"Shh, it's okay," Peyton reassured her, brushing a strand of wet hair from Chloe's face. "You fell into the water, but you're going to be alright. Just try to breathe. Everything's going to be alright now."

She held Chloe and rocked back and forth, as much for her own comfort as Chloe's. As the adrenaline began to fade, Peyton became aware of the coldness seeping into her own bones. She wasn't shivering yet, but she knew it wouldn't be long until hypothermia set in.

How will Sean find us? she wondered. She pulled out her phone, but the waterlogged device refused to turn on. She cast it aside, frustrated. They would just have to follow the river—it had to lead them to civilization eventually.

"Come on," she said to Chloe, gently shaking her shoulders. "You need to get up. We both need to keep moving, get the blood flowing."

Chloe, her head turned to the side and her eyes gazing into the forest, mumbled something.

Peyton leaned closer, frowning. "What was that?"

"We're not alone," Chloe whispered.

Peyton glanced up, puzzled, and suddenly became aware of the low rumble of an engine nearby. There was a vehicle parked at the edge of the woods.

Her heart leaped into her throat. How had Sean found them so quickly? She felt a stirring of relief, and she rose, smiling. Then, as she studied the vehicle more closely, she froze suddenly.

It wasn't an ATV, as she'd assumed, but a golf cart. The killer's golf cart.

Just then, Peyton heard the rustling of leaves to her right. She turned just in time to see a figure sprinting toward her. She threw up her arms as he barreled into her, shoving her backward. She stumbled, tripping on a log, and then she plunged into the cold water of the Ember River, the man above her, holding her down.

CHAPTER TWENTY FIVE

Peyton's chest ached under the man's crushing weight as he pressed her down into the river. The water was shallow, no deeper than a few feet here, but Peyton's attacker had the upper hand, pinning her beneath him.

Panic clawed at her throat as she desperately tried to free herself. Air bubbles escaped her lips, rising toward the surface like silent screams. She could see the man's face, his eyes wild, his expression half-crazed. Her lungs burned with each passing second.

Please, she thought, *I can't let it end like this.*

As her fingers dug into the riverbed, searching for something – anything – to help her escape, a nearby object caught her eye. Instinctively, she reached for it, struggling to grasp the fist-sized rock. Her fingertips brushed against it, yet it remained just out of reach. She felt herself growing faint, losing oxygen, her vision starting to blur around the edges. The unforgiving embrace of darkness closed in on her.

Come on, Peyton. You can do this.

With one last surge of adrenaline, fueled by her will to live, she closed her fingers around the rock. Then, with all her remaining strength, she struck the man across his temple. His grip faltered, and he fell back, releasing her from his hold.

Gasping for breath, Peyton broke the surface, her lungs greedily inhaling the crisp night air. Her heart pounded in her chest as she clung to the rock that had saved her life. The current pulled at her, causing her to sway unsteadily, but she managed to find purchase on the riverbank, digging her heels into the muddy shore.

The only problem was...where had the man gone?

Clouds shifted overhead, momentarily obscuring the moon and plunging everything into an eerie blackness. Peyton searched for the man who had attacked her, but she couldn't see him anywhere. Had he gone back to the golf cart? Was he even now preparing to make his escape?

Then Chloe's scream dragged her back into the moment.

Peyton spun around, her heart racing as she saw Chloe struggling against a tall, burly man. He had his hand over her mouth, muffling her cries for help. Peyton's eyes flared with anger.

"Let her go!" she yelled, brandishing the rock like a weapon. The man turned to face her, his expression twisted with fury. But Peyton didn't flinch. She held the rock tightly, ready to strike if necessary.

For a moment, the man hesitated. Then, with a powerful shove of his arms, he discarded Chloe and turned his full attention on Peyton. Chloe hit the ground hard, and there was a low groan.

"Chloe!" Peyton said, swallowing hard. "Are you okay?"

"Never mind her," the man said. "It's just you and me now."

Peyton's heart raced as she faced the man. The moon emerged from behind the clouds, its light glinting off the man's eyes and revealing his muscled frame as he stepped closer. Peyton held the rock tightly, ready to strike if he made any sudden movements.

A bead of blood ran down the side of the man's face, and he touched it with one fingertip, examining it curiously. "You shouldn't have done that," he said.

Peyton's gaze flickered to the rock in her hand and back to her attacker. "What are you going to do?" she asked, trying to keep her voice steady.

The man's lips twisted into a cruel grin. "I'm going to make you pay for that." With a sudden lunge, he moved toward Peyton.

But Peyton was ready. She dodged out of the way, avoiding his powerful arms. He had to outweigh her by at least eighty pounds, and she knew that if he got a good hold on her, it would be very difficult to escape his grip.

"You're quick," he said, following her. "I like that."

Peyton gritted her teeth, edging backwards. She had to think of a way to turn the tables. There was no one to call for help, no one to intervene. The helicopter was supposed to be scanning this area soon, but there was no guarantee the pilot would see them.

It was just Peyton and the man, locked in a deadly dance.

The man lunged again, and Peyton took a quick step back. Her heel caught on a rock, and she stumbled. The man reached for her, his fingers brushing her arm. Peyton swung the rock, but it merely glanced off the man's shoulder, doing little damage.

"You think you're tough, huh?" he said as she danced back. "You think you can take me down with that little rock?"

Peyton didn't waver. "I'll do whatever it takes to protect myself—and Chloe."

"Ah, Chloe," the man said, looking suddenly thoughtful. "You think you're protecting her? Don't you have any idea what I was doing?"

"Yeah, you were trying to kill her," Peyton said, the words coming out unevenly as her chest shook with shivers.

The man shook his head, looking disgusted. "I was testing her—giving her the chance to save herself."

Suddenly, Peyton recalled her earlier theory about the killer having a savior complex. It seemed she had been right.

"To save herself?" she asked. "By drowning her?"

"I was teaching her to fight back, to stand up for herself."

Peyton narrowed her eyes, not believing a word the man was saying. "That's not teaching, that's torture."

The man laughed, the sound of it making Peyton's skin crawl. "You really don't understand, do you?" he said, taking another step forward. "You and Chloe are weak. You need someone to show you how to be strong."

Peyton felt her anger bubbling up inside her. "Why don't you lead by example and throw yourself in the river?"

The man hesitated, looking at her strangely. "I already did," he said softly. "I nearly drowned when I was a child."

Just then, Peyton became aware of the distant rumble of a helicopter's blades. Help was on the way, after all. She just had to keep this man talking until then.

"How did that happen?" she asked, feigning more interest than she felt.

The man shrugged. "My father pushed me in. He said it was to toughen me up. I guess he didn't care if I drowned."

It was clear that he was deeply disturbed, but Peyton couldn't bring herself to feel sorry for him. Not after what he had done.

"That's terrible," she said, playing along.

The man nodded, his eyes fixed on her. "It changed me. Made me stronger. Made me realize that I was the only one I could rely on. Life is not for the weak and passive, but for the strong and courageous."

His words hung in the cold air, the sound of rushing water from the Ember River providing a chilling soundtrack to their conversation.

"So that's why you drown your victims?" Peyton asked. "You think you're giving them a chance to prove their value?"

"Exactly," the man replied, his eyes narrowing. "I help them find their strength, just like I found mine."

"Then tell me," Peyton asked, "how was Amanda Torres weak? Why did she deserve to die?"

The man hesitated, and for a moment, it seemed as if he might not answer. But then he spoke, his voice filled with conviction. "Amanda was a park ranger, always hiding behind her uniform and authority. She never truly faced any real danger or obstacles. She lived a safe, comfortable life, and that made her weak."

Peyton clenched her fists, anger bubbling within her at the man's twisted logic. "And Kimberly Saunders? Was she weak, too?"

"Kimberly was timid," the man explained, a sickening smile playing on his lips. "She used to be a police officer, but she left that life for the safety of a classroom. She abandoned her courage and chose the easy way out."

"Chloe?"

"Abusive boyfriend. I gave her the chance to leave him, but she wouldn't."

"And you," Peyton said, unable to hold back her indignation. "You think *you're* strong? You think you're somehow better than they are?"

He nodded. "I do. I've proven it."

She shook her head. "No, you haven't. You've proven you prey on vulnerable people to make yourself feel powerful. You don't really want a fair fight—if you did, you'd pick on someone your own size, instead of ambushing those smaller than you."

The man's face twisted with rage, but there was also a flicker of doubt in his eyes. It seemed as if Peyton's words had struck a chord, exposing something raw and painful beneath his surface.

Peyton knew she was taking a big risk, but now that she'd started, she couldn't seem to stop herself.

"You talk about nearly drowning as a child?" she asked. "You think you changed somehow, became stronger because of that incident?"

He said nothing, just went on staring at her, his nostrils flaring.

"You're still that scared little boy," Peyton said, "unable to face the real problems of the world, so instead you create a situation of your own, a situation in which you have the upper hand so you can keep telling yourself you're strong and brave, when in reality you're just a coward so wrapped up in his own insecurities that—"

The man moved at her with frightening speed, charging like a wild animal. She tried to sidestep him, but he caught hold of her, lifting her from the ground and carrying her with him as he splashed into the river. Before she knew it, Peyton was caught in the powerful grasp of the river's current, her arms pinned to her sides as the man held onto her, the cold water surrounding her in a freezing cocoon.

CHAPTER TWENTY SIX

Before Peyton could even begin to free herself, the man forced her head under the water. Peyton's lungs screamed for air, her vision blurry, her body trembling. He was going to drown her, just as he'd drowned his other victims, just like he'd already tried to drown her once.

And this time, she didn't have a rock to strike him with.

Peyton's mind raced, searching for a way to free herself from his iron grip. Her fingers clawed at his hands, desperately seeking purchase, but his hold remained unyielding. They sank further beneath the water, the darkness closing in around them as the current pulled them along. She searched desperately for something to grab hold of, anything to use as a weapon, but her fingers only brushed empty water.

She couldn't – wouldn't – let this be the end, however. As the blackness enveloped her, Peyton summoned every ounce of strength she had left. Kicking her legs with all the force she could muster, she drove her knee into the man's stomach. The water slowed her movements, however, and the blow had little effect. The man only tightened his grip further.

He's going to drown us both, Peyton realized with sudden clarity. *He doesn't care if he dies, so long as I die, too.*

Changing tactics, she decided to find a pressure point to get him to release his hold on her. But where? The man's arms were wrapped tightly around her, keeping her back firmly pressed against him, making it impossible for her to strike him anywhere vital. She tried to kick her feet again, but the water rushed too fast, carrying them along at an incredible pace.

The river's current grew even stronger as they left the shallows of the shore. Peyton's fingers curled around the man's forearms, searching for a pressure point that might give her the leverage she needed to free herself. Finally she found one, located just below his elbow. With all the strength she could muster, she dug her fingers into the soft tissue and pressed down hard, hoping to force him to release his hold.

The man gasped in pain, his grip loosening for a moment. Peyton took advantage of this, twisting and turning in his grasp until she was able to wriggle free. She kicked out at him, her foot connecting with his chest, and then she swam frantically towards the surface.

For a moment, she wasn't sure if she was going to make it. The current was so strong, and her lungs burned with the need for air. But then she broke the surface, gasping.

Now all she needed to do was swim to the shore, get back to Chloe, and—

Just then, she became aware of a loud, hissing sound nearby. She turned her face downstream. Rapids. Peyton could see the churning water ahead, the white foam and spray creating a chaotic and dangerous path through the river.

Her heart sank as she realized there was no way she could swim through the rapids safely. Panic set in, and she began to swim frantically toward the shore, hoping to find a place to climb up and out of the water.

Just then, however, a hand wrapped around her ankle, keeping her from getting away. She wanted to reason with him, to make him understand that he was throwing away his own life along with hers, but he didn't seem to care. She realized that getting away from him wasn't going to work.

She would have to fight him—again.

Peyton twisted around in the water. Rather than trying to break away, however, she threw herself at the man, climbing across his shoulders. She wrapped her arms around his muscular neck and squeezed.

The man's breathing became labored as Peyton's grip tightened around his neck. He tried to free himself from her, but her hold was too strong. He shook his head violently from side to side, trying to throw her off, but she held on with all her might.

He was becoming weaker, his movements slowing down. Peyton could feel his grip on her loosening. Then, suddenly, he relaxed, his body going limp.

Peyton knew that this was her chance to get away from him once and for all. She could simply leave him and swim away, let him suffer the consequences of his own actions.

Could she really live with herself if she did that, though? Could she really let him die, knowing she could've saved him? Although this man had tried to kill her mere moments ago, she couldn't bring herself to let him drown. She was better than that, and she refused to sink to his level. With every fiber of her being, she knew she needed to save him, even if it meant risking her own life.

Gritting her teeth against the biting cold and the relentless current, Peyton tightened her grip around the man's torso and began kicking furiously toward the shore. The weight of his limp body threatened to drag them both under, and she felt her muscles scream in protest with each passing second. She could hear the roar of the rapids growing louder in her ears, a chilling reminder of the danger they faced.

Despite Peyton's best efforts, the current proved too strong, and exhaustion began to take its toll on her body. The rapids loomed ahead, their foamy crests illuminated by the pale moonlight, a horrifying dance of churning water and jagged rocks. Fear coiled around her like a snake, constricting her breaths.

And then, suddenly, Chloe appeared at the edge of the river, just in front of the rapids. Her face was etched with determination as she bent a sapling over, its slender tip reaching down toward the water. The sight of a friendly face filled Peyton's heart with renewed vigor.

With an almost superhuman effort, Peyton steered herself and the unconscious man toward the sapling. She could feel the pull of the rapids growing stronger, her body threatening to give out at any moment. But she refused to let go.

Summoning the last reserves of her strength, Peyton reached out and grasped the end of the sapling with one hand, never letting go of the man with the other. Her knuckles turned white from the force of her grip, but she held on, knowing that their lives depended on it.

"Let him go!" Chloe shouted, her eyes fixed on the man who had caused so much pain. "He doesn't deserve to live!"

Peyton looked at Chloe, her face a mixture of exhaustion and determination. In that moment, she knew that saving this man was not just about stopping a killer; it was about holding onto her own humanity, even in the face of such darkness.

"We have to save him!" Peyton said. Did they really have to have this conversation right now when she could barely hold on?

"He tried to kill us!" Chloe said, her hands shaking as she continued to hold the sapling. "He wouldn't have saved us!"

"And that's what makes us different from him. Now help me, please!"

Chloe hesitated for a moment, her eyes searching Peyton's. Finally, with a nod, she gripped the sapling more tightly and began to help Peyton pull the man out of the river.

Together, they fought against the current, their combined strength gradually overcoming the river's deadly embrace. Slowly, painstakingly, they dragged the man toward the shore, their feet slipping on the rocks beneath the water's surface.

At last, they reached the edge of the river, collapsing onto the rocky bank, their bodies heaving with exhaustion. The man lay on his back, unmoving, water streaming from his soaked clothes.

"Is he...dead?" Chloe asked, her voice quivering with a mixture of fear and hope.

For a moment, there was only silence, punctuated by the sound of their harsh breathing and the rushing water. Then, suddenly, the man coughed violently, spitting up water as he rolled onto his side.

"Guess not," Peyton said grimly, seizing the opportunity to cuff his hands behind his back. She looked down at the groggy, defeated man, her eyes cold and unyielding. "You're under arrest."

Peyton could hardly believe she had survived not one but two attacks from this man. Twice he had held her under the water, and twice she had managed to escape. She was very grateful there would not be a third.

As the adrenaline from the encounter slowly dissipated, Peyton tried to steady her breathing. The sound of water relentlessly rushing past them filled her ears, but she couldn't shake the feeling that their ordeal wasn't over yet. Chloe's eyes flicked around nervously, her arms wrapped around herself as if trying to hold herself together.

"Wait a minute," Chloe said, barely loud enough for Peyton to hear her over the relentless flow of the river. "Do you hear that?"

The distant thud of helicopter blades sliced through the night air, growing louder as the aircraft approached. A searchlight swept across the riverbank, illuminating the trees.

"Over here!" Chloe screamed, jumping up and frantically waving her arms, desperate to catch the helicopter's attention. Her voice cracked with the strain.

The helicopter veered toward them, hovering above as its spotlight focused on the trio below. Peyton squinted against the harsh light, shielding her face with one arm while keeping a firm grip on the subdued killer with the other. She could see the figure in the helicopter, silhouetted against the moonlit sky.

He began to rappel down, his movements swift and confident. His boots hit the shore with a soft thud, and he immediately trotted over to them, weapon drawn.

"Are you alright?" Sean asked, looking over the three of them with worried eyes.

Peyton felt a dam of emotion threatening to burst free, but not until Sam had taken charge of the killer did she allow it to break. As the first sobs came, Chloe touched her arm. Peyton turned, and the two women threw their arms around one another, clutching one another as they held on through their shared grief.

And beside them, the river went on murmuring a song that had no end.

CHAPTER TWENTY SEVEN

Peyton shivered uncontrollably, her wet clothes sticking to her skin as she huddled on the bank of the Ember River. The cold air gnawed at her bones, turning her lips a shade of blue, and her teeth chattered noisily.

The river may get me, after all, she thought with a despairing kind of good humor.

The scene around her was a flurry of activity, a pair of ambulances and several park ranger vehicles occupying the riverbank, their lights glimmering across the water. Apparently, there was a major access road nearby, allowing the vehicles to traverse the open terrain along the bank of the river. Peyton was profoundly grateful for this. There wouldn't have been enough room on the helicopter for all of them to leave together, and she didn't want anyone getting left behind on this stretch of lonely wilderness.

She looked up, squinting against the glare of the vehicles' headlights, as Sean approached with a heavy blanket in his arms. His face was a mixture of concern and relief as he draped the warm fabric around her shoulders, offering a small, reassuring smile.

"That should help a bit," he said.

"Thank you," Peyton whispered through chattering teeth, grateful for both the warmth of the blanket and his comforting presence. She wrapped it tighter around herself, taking solace in its embrace.

Just then, Chloe approached them, arm tightly linked around an older woman who bore a striking resemblance to her. Both were visibly shaken but carried a sense of determination in their eyes. The woman's graying hair framed her careworn features, while Chloe's dark curls cascaded down her back, creating a stark contrast between mother and daughter.

"This is my mom, Jane," Chloe said, her voice trembling slightly. "Mom, this woman is the ranger who—" Before she could say anything further, Jane moved forward and threw her arms around Peyton, tears streaming down her face.

"Thank you so much for saving my Chloe," Jane sobbed. "I don't know what I would have done without her."

Peyton hesitated, unsure of how to respond to such raw emotion and gratitude. Her instincts had kicked in when she saw Chloe in danger, and she knew she would do it again in a heartbeat. But now, faced with the reality of what she had done, she felt a strange mix of humility and pride.

"Y-you're welcome," she stammered, her voice barely audible over her chattering teeth. "I'm just glad I could help."

As the embrace between Jane and Peyton continued, Sean stepped back, giving them some space. His eyes briefly met Peyton's, and he offered her a small smile before turning to Chloe. "You okay?" he asked gently, placing a hand on her shoulder.

Chloe nodded, her eyes downcast. "I will be," she said quietly. "Thanks to both of you."

Sean's gaze lingered on her for a moment longer before turning back to Peyton and the older woman. "We should get you all warmed up and checked out," he said, glancing over at the ambulance. "They'll take care of you there."

"I have to know something," Chloe said. "What will happen to him now?" She gestured toward the handcuffed man in the back of one of the park ranger vehicles. He was slumped forward, his head hanging forward, a picture of defeat and resignation. Seeing this, Peyton felt pity for him, but also a sense of relief that he had been caught before he could do any more harm.

"He'll be taken into custody by the authorities," Sean said. "They'll investigate further and gather evidence. He'll face charges for his crimes, including murder, attempted murder, and kidnapping. It won't bring back those he hurt, but it's a start."

Chloe nodded, her expression a mixture of relief and determination. "Good. He deserves whatever punishment he gets." Jane squeezed her daughter's shoulder, offering a solemn nod of agreement.

"Take care, both of you," Peyton said softly, watching as Chloe and Jane walked away, their arms still linked together as if drawing strength from one another. As the pair receded into the distance, Peyton couldn't help but feel grateful that they were safe.

Sean, who had been standing silently beside her, finally spoke up. "I heard you saved the man after knocking him out," he said, his tone curious yet tinged with admiration. "Why'd you do that? You could've just let him drown in the river—nobody would've been the wiser."

Peyton sighed, her breath visible in the chilly air as she wrapped the blanket tighter around herself. "I couldn't just let him die," she said.

"Even though he's a monster, letting him drown would make me no better than he is. He needs to face justice for what he's done."

Sean nodded thoughtfully. Peyton had the impression that he wasn't entirely sure what decision he would have made, but that he respected her decision nonetheless.

"Any idea why he did what he did?" he asked.

"According to his twisted logic, he was testing them—picking women he thought were weak, then trying to drown them."

"*Trying*?"

"He wanted them to fight back, to prove they weren't as weak as they appeared. If they succeeded, he would let them go. If not..." Peyton shivered.

Sean shook his head dismissively. "That doesn't make any sense. Where'd he come up with something like that?"

"His father nearly drowned him when he was a child, and apparently the incident taught him the need to be strong. He seems to believe only the strong deserve to live."

"Guess we'll have to put Arnold on suicide watch, then, considering all this." Sean shook his head, looking suddenly weary.

"Arnold?" Peyton asked, surprised.

Sean took a deep breath before answering. "Arnold Ipswitch. One of the other rangers recognized him. According to the ranger, Arnold is a bit of a drifter. He's been connected to several other violent incidents, but nothing quite like this. He has a history of mental health issues, which may have played a role in his actions tonight. But rest assured, regardless of what series of events led to tonight, he'll be facing serious consequences for what he's done. He's going away for a long time."

Peyton nodded, grateful for the information. It was some small comfort to know that Arnold would face justice, and that his reign of terror was finally at an end. Her gaze lingered on the vehicle containing Arnold, and she couldn't help but feel a strange mixture of pity and disgust at the thought of what he had done.

"So," Sean said, studying her, "want to tell me what happened here? I still haven't heard your side of things."

She swallowed hard, shivering again. "Honestly, I'm tired and freezing, and I could probably eat a cow at this point. And I'd kill someone for a hot drink."

"Let's head into town then," Sean said. "There's a diner not too far from here that should still be open. They make amazing hot chocolate."

Peyton nodded, grateful. "I'd like that."

"Then let's go." Sean smiled, offering her his hand. She hesitated, looking up at him. She thought of how she'd felt, seeing him descending from the helicopter—the reassurance that she was no longer alone, that help had arrived. She took his hand, feeling a sense of comfort in his touch.

"That hot chocolate had better be worth it," she said with a smile.

***

As the rich, warm liquid of the tomato soup slid down Peyton's throat, it seemed to radiate warmth throughout her entire body, chasing away the chill that had settled deep within her bones. With each bite of the crispy, gooey sandwich, she felt her strength returning, and the traumatic events of the night began to recede ever so slightly.

Glad we stopped by the hotel so I could change into some dry clothes, she thought. *Otherwise, I'd have frozen to death by now.*

"Feeling better?" Sean asked, watching her with an expression that was half concern, half amusement.

"Much better," she replied, her voice stronger now. "Thanks for bringing me here."

"Least I could do after everything you've been through tonight. Jumping off that cliff to save Chloe—" He shook his head as if he couldn't quite believe it. "That's remarkable."

Peyton shrugged modestly. "It just seemed like the right thing to do."

They ate in companionable silence, the only sounds being the clink of silverware against plates and the murmuring of other patrons. Peyton noticed Sean's gaze lingering on her, a faint smile playing at the corners of his lips. She raised an eyebrow, curious about what thoughts were running through his mind.

"What's so funny?" she asked, wiping her mouth with a napkin.

"Nothing," he answered, shaking his head. "I just can't believe you jumped off that cliff to save Chloe. Maybe *you're* the one with the savior complex."

Peyton laughed, the tension in her chest easing slightly. "Maybe I do. But if it means saving someone innocent, I think it's worth it."

Sean nodded, his expression growing more serious. "I understand that. It's just...not everyone would have made the same choice. It takes a lot of courage to do what you did."

Peyton paused, considering his words. "I guess I've always believed that helping the innocent is important because they don't deserve the pain and suffering they're going through. They need someone to stand up for them when no one else will." She thought back to her own childhood, the loss of her parents, and the years she'd spent in the foster system, feeling helpless and alone. "I know what it's like to be defenseless, needing someone to look out for you."

"Well," Sean said, chewing his last bite of burger and chasing it with a swallow of beer, "it's clear that you've certainly made a difference in Chloe's life. You saved her tonight, and I have a feeling that she'll be grateful for that for a long time."

Peyton smiled, feeling a sense of pride swell in her chest. "I hope so."

Sean's eyes wandered, studying the few other patrons scattered around the room.

Peyton finished her bowl of tomato bisque, then wiped her mouth with a napkin and asked, "So, what happened with you and Ed Davis?"

Sean leaned back in his chair, a grin spreading across his face. "Well, it took some convincing, but I finally managed to get him to come out of that cave. You should have seen him—or smelled him, rather. If you thought that cave smelled like weed..."

Peyton chuckled. "What was his alibi?"

"Turns out he was just hiding out there because he'd had a fight with his girlfriend and needed some space. As far as having the shoe…" Sean shrugged. "His girlfriend said he was kind of weird like that. Very active fantasy life, if you know what I mean."

The moment of levity passed, and Sean's smile faded. He seemed to consider his words carefully before speaking again. "Can I share something with you?"

"Of course." Peyton studied her partner's eyes, curious as to where this was going.

"I haven't really talked much about this, but after Gabriela died, I almost quit the NPS. I thought I couldn't handle losing someone else I cared about."

A pang of sympathy pierced Peyton's heart as she saw the vulnerability in Sean's eyes. She knew how difficult it must be for him to share something so personal, and she felt honored that he trusted her enough to do so.

"I'm sorry you had to go through that," she said. "It's hard to lose someone, especially when you work so closely together. But I think it's important to remember the good times and the difference you made together."

He looked down at the table, then back into her eyes. "You're right. It's just hard sometimes, you know? But I decided to stay because I believe in what we do—protecting people and preserving these wild places."

Peyton nodded, grateful for how he was beginning to open up with her. She found herself hoping they might actually become friends, not just colleagues, which would make working together much easier.

Sean leaned back, his chair creaking. He sighed. "You look exhausted," he said. "Want me to take you back to your hotel?"

She nodded. "I'd appreciate that." She could fly back to her cabin in Virginia tomorrow. Tonight, however, she needed all the sleep she could get.

They both rose. Sean paid for their meals, putting it on a work card, and then he joined Peyton as they walked out into the cool, dark night. They said nothing as they got into the SUV. Peyton, warm and full, felt her eyelids drooping as she snuggled into the seat. Sean started the engine, and they drove off into the quiet streets of the small town.

As they drove, Peyton watched the passing scenery, the streetlights casting an orange glow on the buildings they passed. The silence between them was comfortable, and she found herself feeling grateful for Sean's company. He was someone she could trust, and that was a rare thing in her line of work.

Before she knew it, they had arrived at her hotel. Sean pulled up to the curb, then turned off the engine. He turned to her, his eyes soft. "Get some rest, Peyton. You earned it."

She hesitated, choosing her words carefully. "Thank you. Not just for tonight, but for everything along the river. I don't know what I would have done without you."

He shook his head modestly. "I didn't get there in time to save you, though."

"Maybe not," she admitted, her voice softening. "But without you showing up when you did, who knows how long the three of us would've been stranded out there, soaked to the bone and freezing cold. So thank you."

"Anytime, Peyton," he replied, a small smile gracing his lips. "You're welcome."

Stepping out of the SUV, Peyton gazed at the quaint, two-story hotel before them, its exterior adorned with twinkling fairy lights. The light emanating from within seemed to promise comfort and safety after the harrowing events of the day.

"Take care, Sean," Peyton said as she waved goodbye to him. His SUV pulled away, leaving her standing in front of the hotel, the cool evening air enveloping her. She watched his taillights disappear into the night and felt a warmth in her chest, knowing their friendship had grown stronger through the challenges they'd faced together.

With a deep breath, Peyton pushed open the heavy wooden doors of the hotel, feeling the warmth from inside spill out onto the cold pavement. She was ready for a hot shower and a long sleep before heading back to Virginia in the morning. Tomorrow would be a new day with new challenges and opportunities.

For now, it was time to rest.

EPILOGUE

"Thought you'd never come back to sort through your folks' stuff," Owen said as he piloted the old pickup truck through the warren of storage units. "To be honest, though, I was relieved to get your call. I could really use that storage unit for other things."

It was afternoon, a day after Peyton had wrapped up the investigation involving the drownings in Great Smoky Mountains National Park, and Peyton was sitting in the passenger seat of Owen's truck, the leather cracked and sun-tinted beneath her. The radio was playing a country tune, something about a dog and a truck and a favorite tackle box, but it was too low for Peyton to follow the lyrics.

A few years had passed since she'd last worked with Owen back when they were both in the FBI, he an analyst and she a field agent. He'd put on weight since then, his once-athletic body now soft and round. She'd also heard that he'd retired early, citing stress-related health issues. But as she looked at him now, she saw a hint of the same sharpness in his eyes that had always made him such a valuable asset to their team.

"Sorry it's taken me so long," she said, feeling a twinge of guilt for the burden she'd inadvertently placed on him. "I appreciate you looking after everything for so long."

"Ah, don't mention it," he said with a dismissive wave. "What are friends for?"

Peyton smiled, then glanced out the window at the rows upon rows of storage units stretching across the vast, gravel-covered lot. Each unit was marked with a faded number painted on its metal door, creating a maze-like effect as they drove deeper into the property. Somewhere in this sea of forgotten belongings, her parents' possessions were waiting, laden with secrets.

As the silence lengthened, Peyton thought back to what Owen had said and realized he was probably expecting her to empty out the entire unit. She turned to him, wanting to set the record straight. "I hope you don't think I'm planning on taking everything out of the storage unit," she said.

His face fell with disappointment. "Then what are you here for?"

"I need to find something," she said, her voice competing with the hum of the truck's engine. "I don't know exactly what it is, but I'm hoping I'll recognize it when I see it."

Owen's brows furrowed, his curiosity piqued despite his disappointment. "What do you mean?"

Peyton hesitated, unsure of how much she should reveal. She glanced out the window, her gaze lost in the late afternoon sun that filtered through the trees lining the storage facility. The shadows cast by their branches danced playfully across the ground, oblivious to the weight of the past that loomed over her.

"Have you ever heard of the Red Pine Cabin in Sprucewood Springs?" she asked Owen, her mind drifting back to the message her father had left with Rex Albright, the park ranger. Owen shook his head, clearly puzzled.

"No, I can't say I have. What does that have to do with your parents' belongings?"

Peyton sighed, deciding to trust Owen with her thoughts. "My father mentioned it in a message he left with a park ranger before my parents died. I think there might be a connection between that cabin and their murder. If I can find something related to it in the storage unit, maybe I can finally get some answers."

The gravity of her words hung heavily between them as Owen absorbed the information. He nodded slowly, understanding dawning on his face. "If there's anything that can help you, I'm sure it's in there. And if you need any help, I'm here for you."

"Thank you," Peyton said. "As far as the unit—"

Owen waved a hand. "Forget about it."

"No, I want to pay for it. I appreciate that you've let it slide, but I can't take advantage of your generosity any longer. I'll either make a plan to take everything back, or I'll start paying rent like everyone else."

He glanced at her, a hint of gratitude in his eyes. "That would mean a lot, actually. I didn't want to make you feel bad, but my wife's been fighting this bacterial infection, and the cost of medicine and treatments has been piling up. We could really use the extra income right now."

Peyton reached out and placed a hand on his arm. "I'm sorry to hear that. Let me know how much I owe you, and I'll take care of it as soon as possible."

Owen nodded, then pulled the truck to a stop in front of one of the units. The corrugated metal walls were slightly rusted, and weeds poked through cracks in the concrete floor. A sense of anticipation seized Peyton as her heartbeat quickened. It had been years since she last stepped foot in this place, and now it housed the memories of her parents—and possibly the key to solving their murder.

"This is the one," Owen said, pointing to the faded '13' painted on the door.

As they got out of the truck, Owen fumbled with his keyring, searching for the right key among the many that jangled together. Peyton watched him, the Red Pine Cabin looming large in her thoughts, its secrets teasing at the edges of her consciousness.

"Got it," Owen muttered, holding up the key before sliding it into the lock. He turned it with a satisfying click and began to roll up the metal door.

"Wait," Peyton said, placing a hand on his arm. "I...I think I'd like to be alone in there, if that's okay."

Owen paused, his eyes filled with understanding. "Of course. Just give me a call if you need anything. I'll be in the truck."

"Thank you," she murmured, grateful for his support and sensitivity.

Peyton watched Owen climb back into his truck, the door closing behind him with a soft thud. She took a deep breath, steeling herself for the flood of memories that awaited her within the storage unit. Her hand gripped the metal handle, and she slowly raised the door, revealing the hidden world inside.

The bright sunlight cast a warm glow over the items that filled the unit, each one a piece of her parents' lives. Antique furniture sat patiently in the corners, waiting to be used once more: a beautifully carved wooden rocking chair, a set of mahogany bookshelves laden with dust-covered tomes, and an ornate dresser with brass handles gleaming faintly in the low light. Rugs were rolled up and leaned against the walls, their once vibrant colors muted by time.

Peyton stepped inside, her heart heavy with nostalgia and grief, but also brimming with determination. As she walked through the unit, her fingers traced the surfaces of the objects around her, connecting with her past through touch.

She came across a small, worn teddy bear—Mr. Cuddles, a constant companion throughout her childhood. The distant sound of her mother's laughter echoed in her ears as she lifted it gently, cradling it in her hands before placing it back down on a nearby trunk.

The scent of cedarwood and pine filled her nostrils as she opened the lid of an old chest, revealing a collection of her father's fishing gear. She could almost feel the cool breeze that blew through the trees lining the riverbanks where they had spent countless hours casting lines and reeling in their catch. Blinking away tears, Peyton closed the chest, the sound of the latch clicking into place like a farewell.

As she continued her exploration, she uncovered more pieces of her past: photo albums filled with images of smiling faces, her mother's china set meticulously wrapped in newspaper, and a ragged quilt that had been lovingly sewn together by her grandmother. Each item brought forth a rush of memories, both joyful and painful, but all precious to Peyton.

Though it hurt to be surrounded by these reminders of her parents' lives, there was also a sense of comfort in revisiting the moments they had shared. It was as if she could feel their presence within the storage unit, guiding her through the painful process of unearthing the truth behind their deaths.

As Peyton searched for any clue that might lead her to the Red Pine Cabin and the answers she sought, she allowed herself to be embraced by the warmth of her memories. The nostalgia wrapped itself around her like a familiar blanket, providing solace and strength as she faced the daunting task ahead. For now, amidst the relics of her past, she found a moment of peace and clarity—a chance to heal, even if only briefly, before resuming her relentless pursuit of justice.

Fortifying herself with a series of deep breaths, Peyton pulled out her phone, navigated to the recording her father had sent to Rex Albright, and pressed play. The familiar sound of his voice washed over her like a balm, momentarily transporting her back to her childhood. She closed her eyes and let herself be enveloped by the memories evoked by the items surrounding her and the comforting timbre of her father's voice.

Inhaling deeply, the scents of aged wood and leather filled her nostrils, mingling with the faint aroma of her mother's favorite perfume, still lingering after all these years. It was as if Peyton were standing in their cabin once more, surrounded by her parents' laughter and love.

Tears threatened to spill from the corners of her eyes, the longing for those simpler times clawing at her heart.

Listening to the message, her father's voice crackled through the speaker, slightly distorted but familiar all the same. As the recording played, Peyton could almost feel the warmth of the fireplace in their old cabin, the sensation of sitting on her father's lap as he told her stories about his adventures in the wilderness.

The recording came to an end, and Peyton opened her eyes, wiping away the tears that had managed to escape. She couldn't afford to lose herself in nostalgia; there was work to be done. A clue hidden somewhere in this storage unit might hold the key to unraveling her parents' murder, and she was determined to find it.

"Hey, Peyton," Owen said, breaking the silence. Startled, she turned to see him standing at the entrance of the storage unit. "I promised a friend I'd drive over and feed their dogs while they're gone. If you're going to be here a while, I can come back and pick you up later. Think you'll be long?"

Peyton's gaze swept over the rows of antique furniture, faded photographs, and mementos that had once filled their family cabin. Each artifact seemed to hum with memories, beckoning her to uncover a secret that had been buried for years.

Who had killed her parents, and why? Had they known their killer? Had they been targeted deliberately, or was it random? And what did any of it have to do with the Red Pine Cabin?

Peyton didn't know the answer to any of those questions. She did know, however, that she had come too far to give up now. One way or another, she wasn't going to leave until she had the answer she sought.

"Go ahead, Owen," she said in a voice that was both soft and steely. "I'm going to be here for as long as it takes."

NOW AVAILABLE!

WHAT'S GONE
(A Peyton Risk Suspense Thriller—Book Four)

Amidst the untamed swamps of Louisiana, a relentless killer strangles victims with vines, leaving behind ominous sculptures crafted from twigs. National Parks Officer Peyton Risk, an expert at solving homicides within the National parks, is needed to catch him and decode his mysterious symbols. With Peyton's deep knowledge of the wilderness, she can track a killer as no one can. Yet this time, she must wonder if it is *she* who is being tracked....

WHAT'S GONE (A Peyton Risk Suspense Thriller—Book 4) is Book #4 in a new series by mystery and suspense author Ella Swift.

Raised in the heart of the mountains by avid outdoors enthusiasts, Peyton followed in her parents' footsteps and became an expert in the natural world. Until, at just 12 years old, an idyllic family camping trip in their favorite national park turned into a nightmare. Her parents were brutally murdered, the killer vanished into the wild, and the case went cold.

Despite being haunted by the unsolved deaths of her parents, Peyton turned her trauma into determination, studying environmental science in college and becoming a respected National Parks Officer. Peyton's unique perspective blends an intuition for the outdoors with a sharp intellect that allows her to decipher secrets hidden within the parks—set on ensuring that no other family endures the same pain that hers did.

But will she find herself the next victim claimed in the park's unforgiving wilderness?

A page-turning and harrowing thriller featuring a brilliant and tortured protagonist, the PEYTON RISK series is a riveting mystery, packed with non-stop action, suspense, twists and turns, revelations, and driven by a breakneck pace that will keep you flipping pages late into the night.

Future books in the series are also available!

Ella Swift

Ella Swift is author of the PEYTON RISK mystery series, comprising five books (and counting).

An avid reader and lifelong fan of the mystery and thriller genres, Ella loves to hear from you, so please feel free to visit ellaswiftauthor.com to learn more and stay in touch.

BOOKS BY ELLA SWIFT

PEYTON RISK MYSTERY SERIES
WHAT'S HIS (Book #1)
WHAT'S LEFT (Book #2)
WHAT'S WISHED (Book #3)
WHAT'S GONE (Book #4)
WHAT'S MINE (Book #5)

Made in United States
Orlando, FL
12 September 2024

51454886R00093